Val

‖‖‖‖‖‖‖‖‖‖‖‖‖‖‖‖‖‖
✓ Y0-AAR-563

HÄGAR
The Horrible

PILLAGE
IDIOT

by
DiK
BROWNE

TOR

A TOM DOHERTY ASSOCIATES BOOK

This is a work of fiction. All the characters and events portrayed in this book are fictional, and any resemblance to real people or incidents is purely coincidental.

HAGAR THE HORRIBLE: PILLAGE IDIOT

First TOR printing: May 1986

A TOR Book

Published by Tom Doherty Associates
49 West 24 Street
New York, N.Y. 10010

ISBN: 0-812-50605-7   Can. ISBN: 0-812-50606-5

Printed in the United States

0 9 8 7 6 5 4 3 2

BIG MOUTH

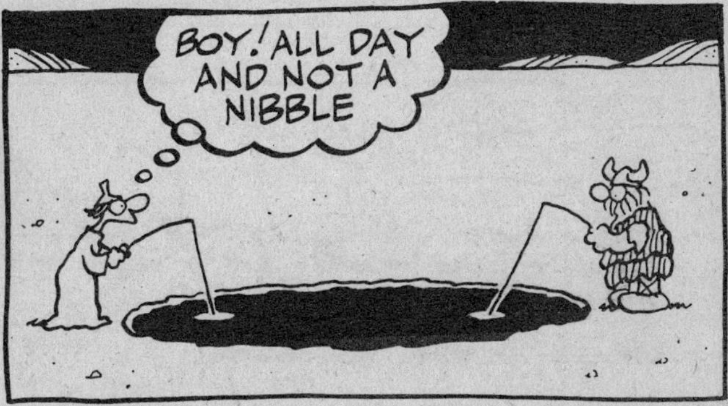
BOY! ALL DAY AND NOT A NIBBLE

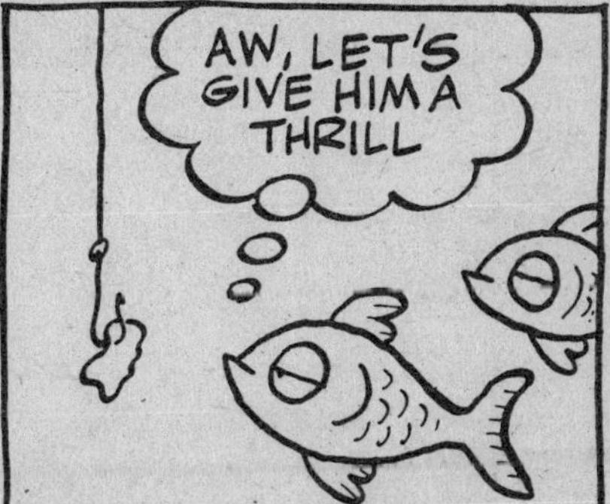
AW, LET'S GIVE HIM A THRILL

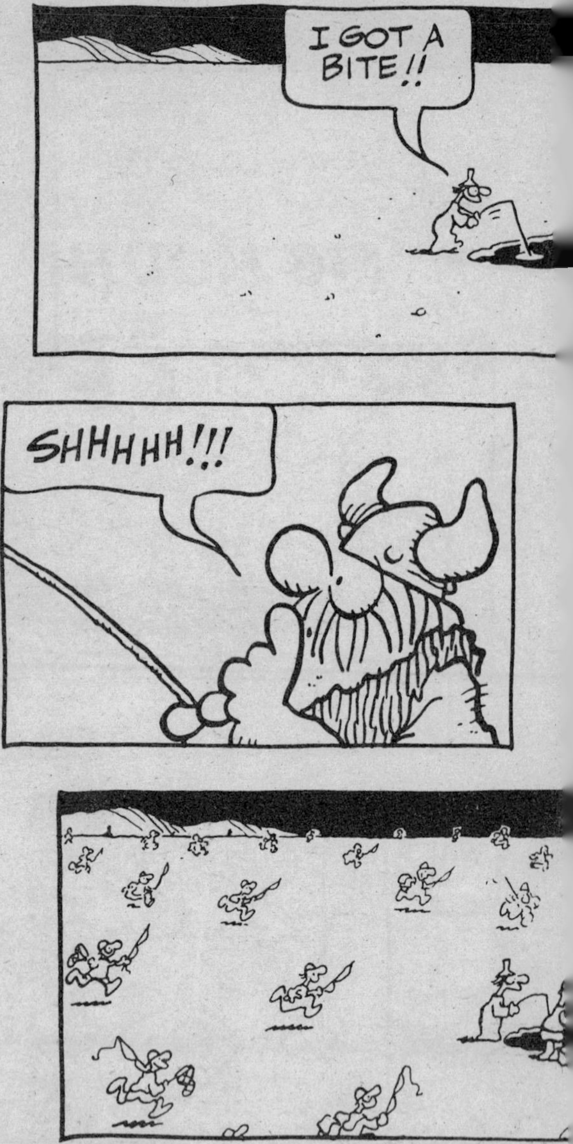
I GOT A BITE!!
SHHHHH!!!

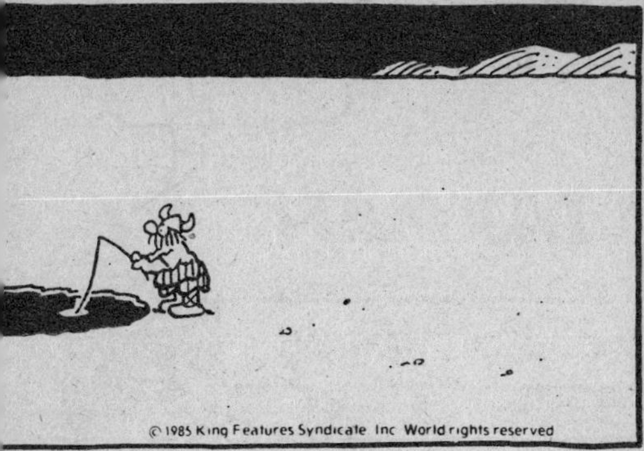
© 1985 King Features Syndicate Inc World rights reserved

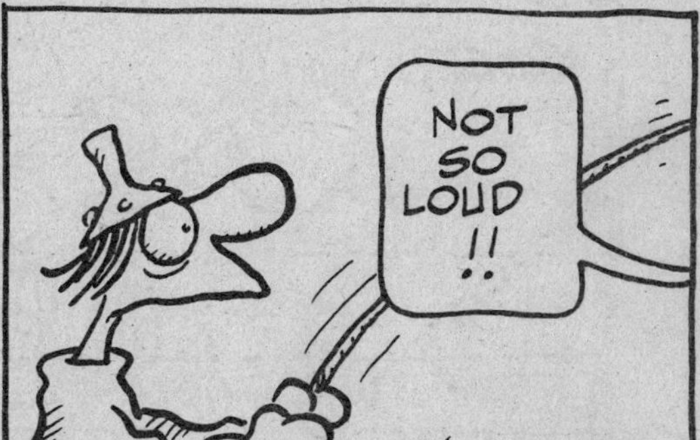
NOT SO LOUD!!
DIK BROWNE 9-1

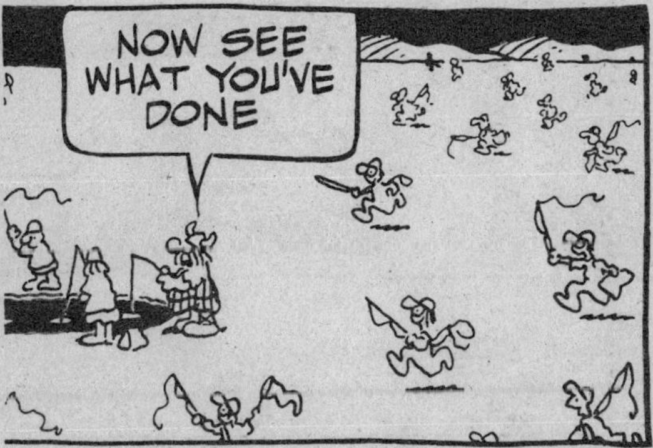
NOW SEE WHAT YOU'VE DONE

TAXMAN

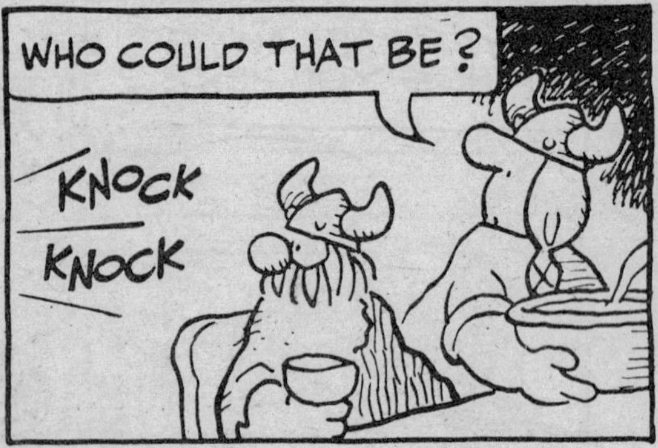
WHO COULD THAT BE?
KNOCK
KNOCK

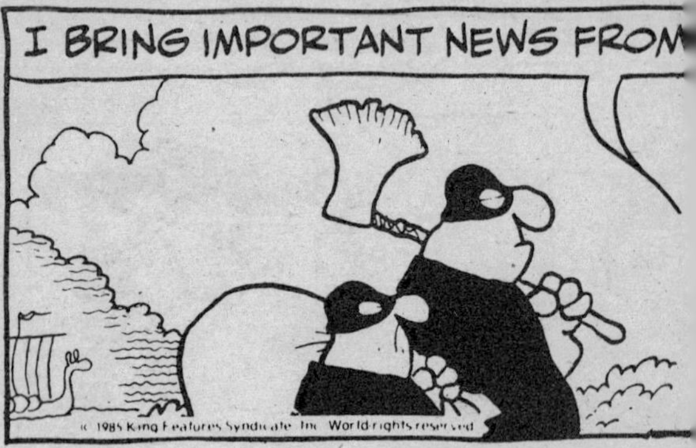
I BRING IMPORTANT NEWS FROM
© 1985 King Features Syndicate, Inc. World rights reserved

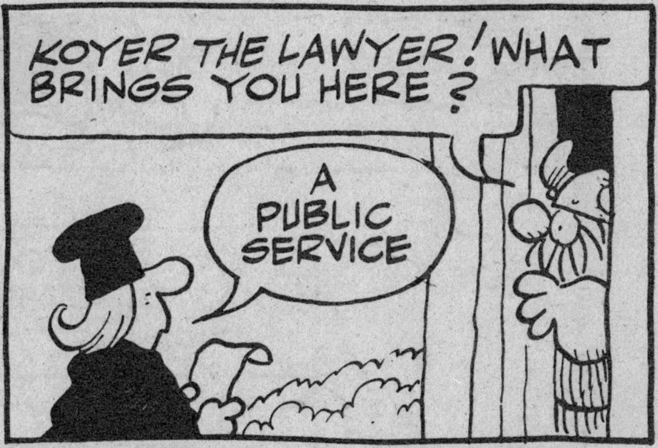
KOYER THE LAWYER! WHAT BRINGS YOU HERE?
A PUBLIC SERVICE

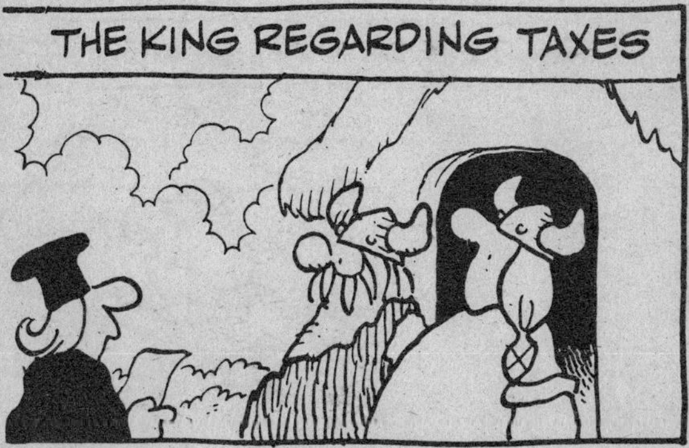
THE KING REGARDING TAXES

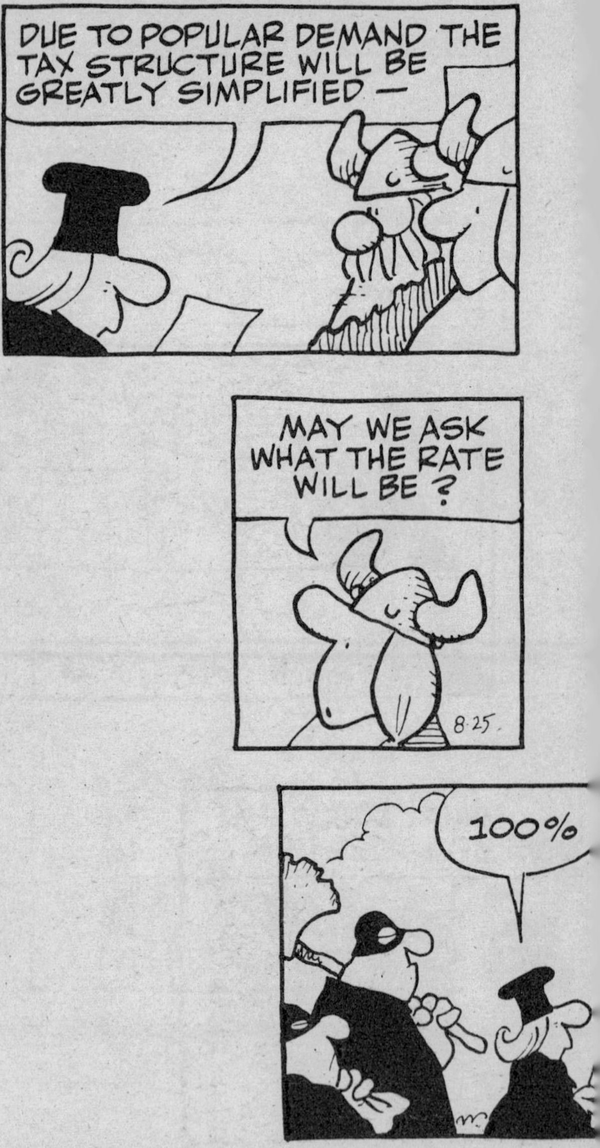
DUE TO POPULAR DEMAND THE TAX STRUCTURE WILL BE GREATLY SIMPLIFIED —
MAY WE ASK WHAT THE RATE WILL BE ?
8·25
100%

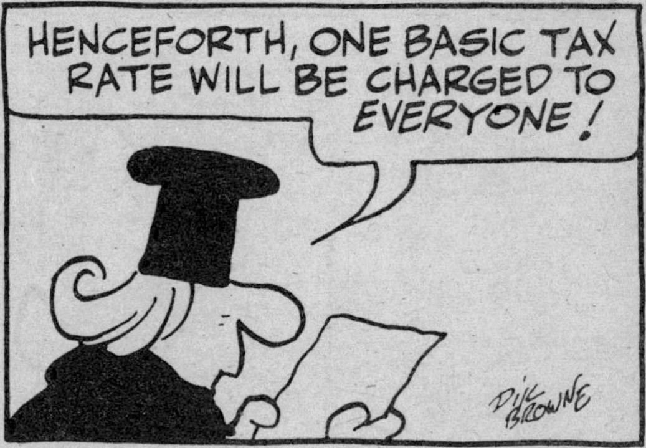
HENCEFORTH, ONE BASIC TAX RATE WILL BE CHARGED TO EVERYONE!
DIK BROWNE

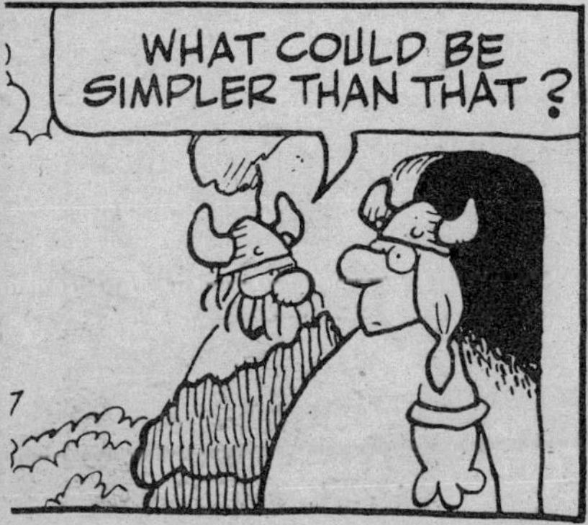
WHAT COULD BE SIMPLER THAN THAT?

FOND FAREWELL

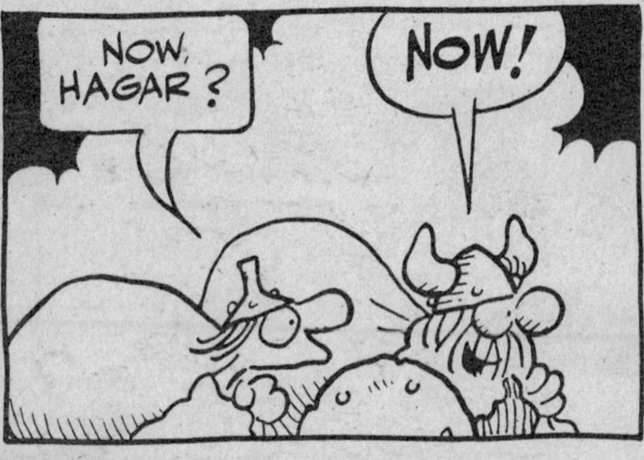
NOW, HAGAR ?
NOW!

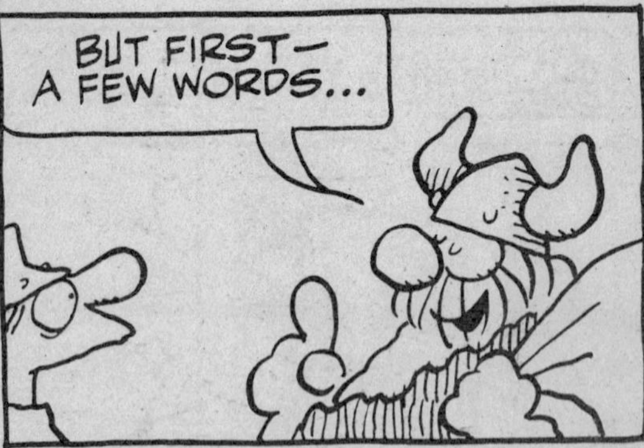
BUT FIRST— A FEW WORDS...

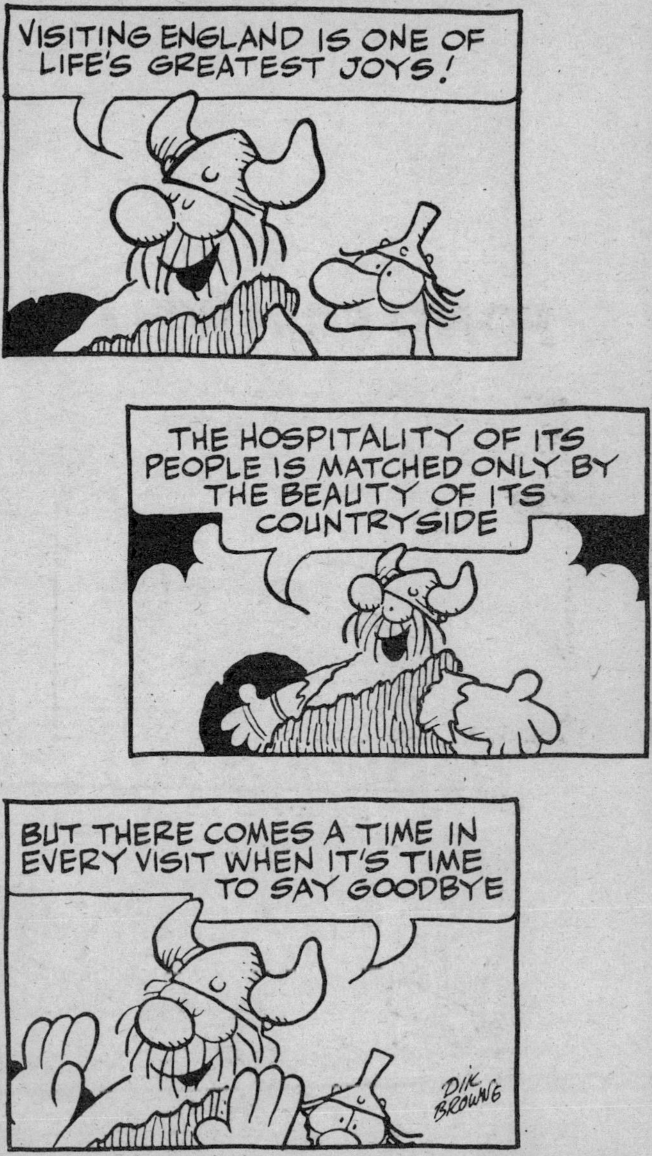
VISITING ENGLAND IS ONE OF LIFE'S GREATEST JOYS!
THE HOSPITALITY OF ITS PEOPLE IS MATCHED ONLY BY THE BEAUTY OF ITS COUNTRYSIDE
BUT THERE COMES A TIME IN EVERY VISIT WHEN IT'S TIME TO SAY GOODBYE
DIK BROWNE

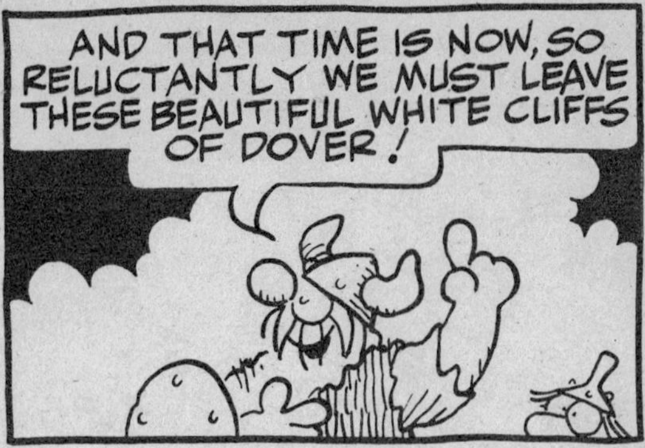
AND THAT TIME IS NOW, SO RELUCTANTLY WE MUST LEAVE THESE BEAUTIFUL WHITE CLIFFS OF DOVER!

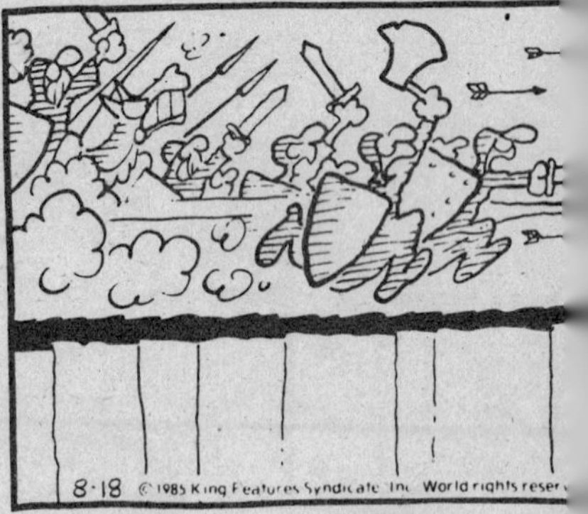
8·18 © 1985 King Features Syndicate Inc World rights reserv

GROWING PAINS

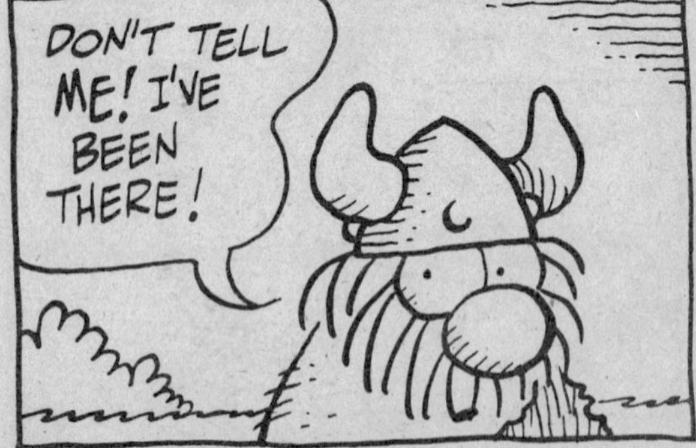
DON'T TELL ME! I'VE BEEN THERE!

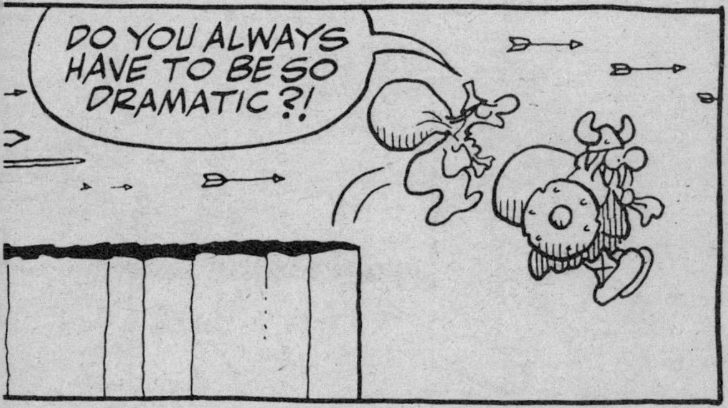
DO YOU ALWAYS HAVE TO BE SO DRAMATIC?!

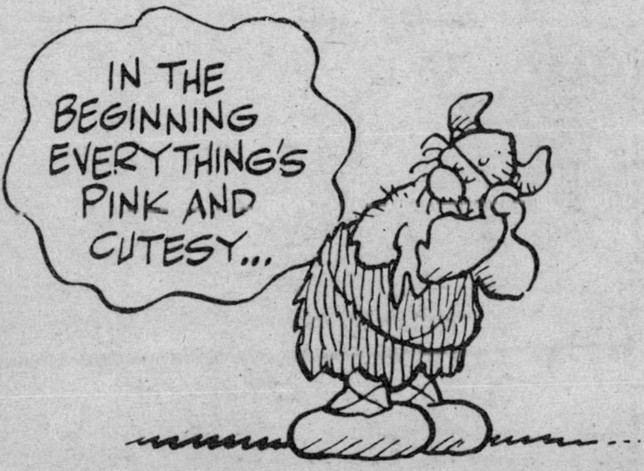
IN THE BEGINNING EVERYTHING'S PINK AND CUTESY...

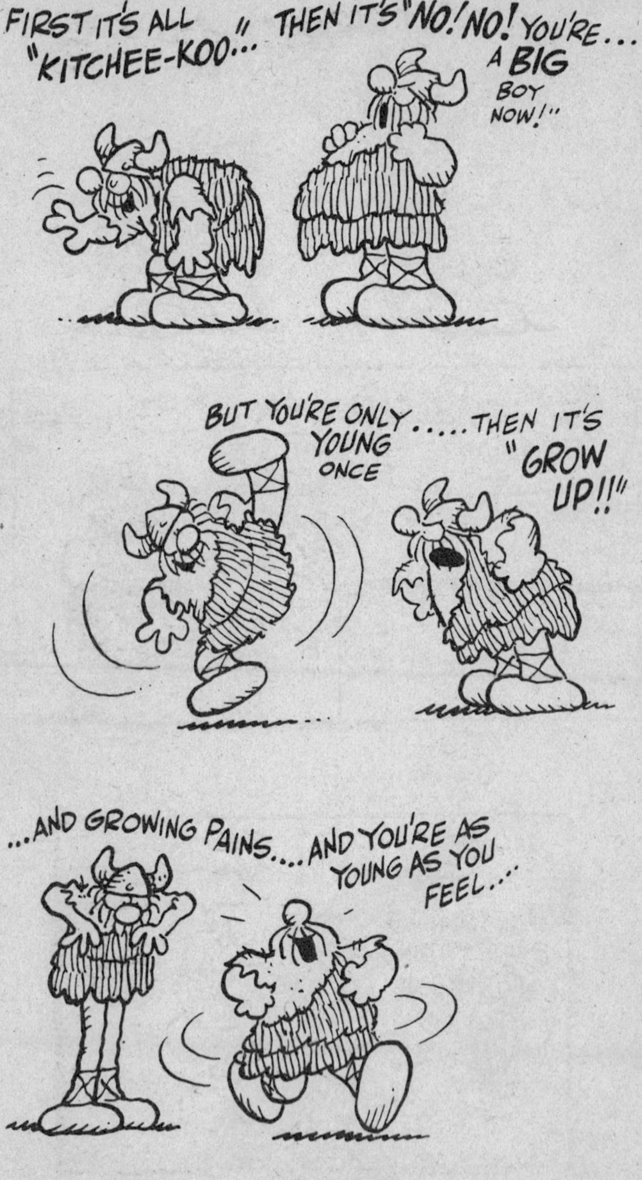
FIRST IT'S ALL "KITCHEE-KOO..."
THEN IT'S "NO! NO! YOU'RE... A BIG BOY NOW!"
BUT YOU'RE ONLY YOUNG ONCE
.....THEN IT'S "GROW UP!!"
...AND GROWING PAINS....
AND YOU'RE AS YOUNG AS YOU FEEL...

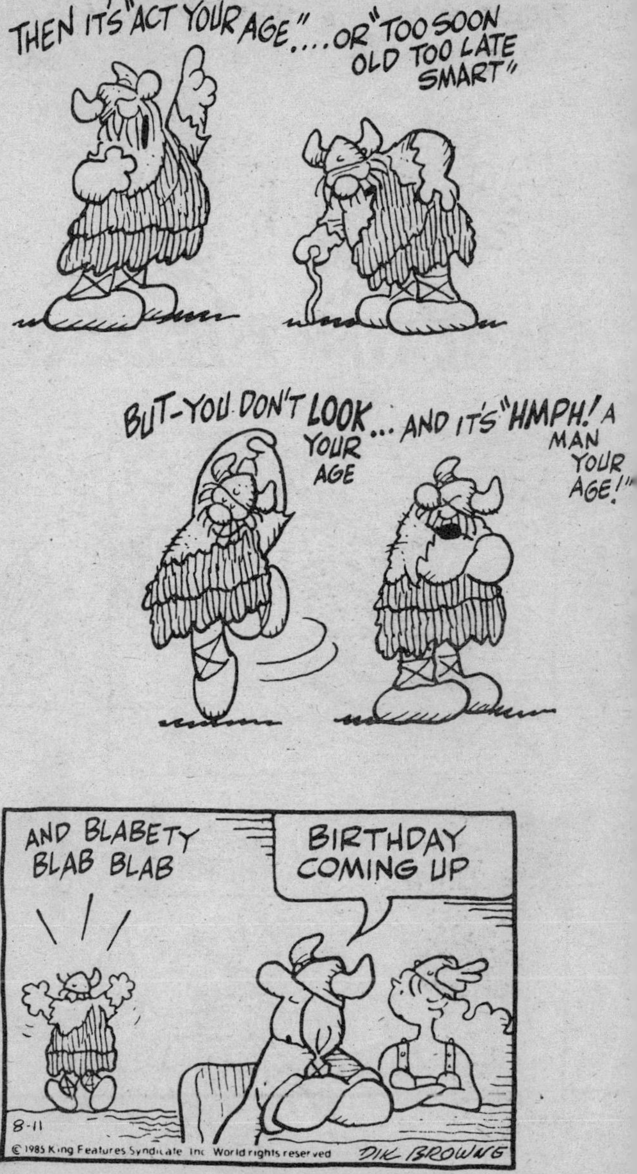
THEN IT'S "ACT YOUR AGE"... OR "TOO SOON OLD TOO LATE SMART"
BUT-YOU DON'T LOOK YOUR AGE
... AND IT'S "HMPH! A MAN YOUR AGE!"
AND BLABETY BLAB BLAB
BIRTHDAY COMING UP
8-11
© 1985 King Features Syndicate Inc World rights reserved
DIK BROWNE

WALKIN' THE DOG

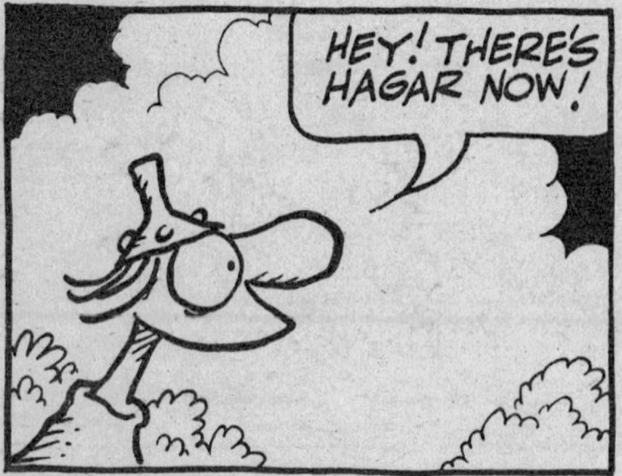
HEY! THERE'S HAGAR NOW!

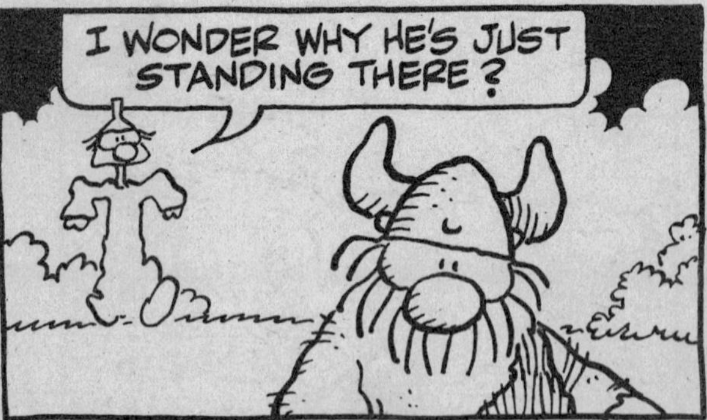
I WONDER WHY HE'S JUST STANDING THERE?

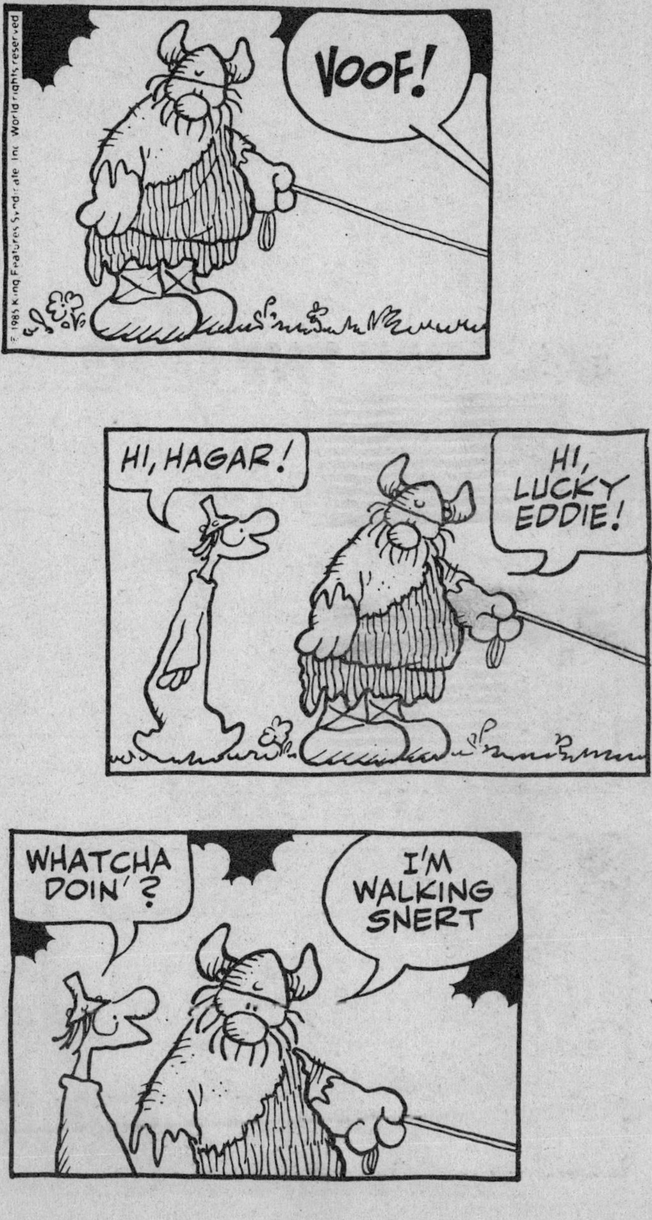
© 1985 King Features Syndicate Inc World rights reserved
VOOF!
HI, HAGAR!
HI, LUCKY EDDIE!
WHATCHA DOIN'?
I'M WALKING SNERT

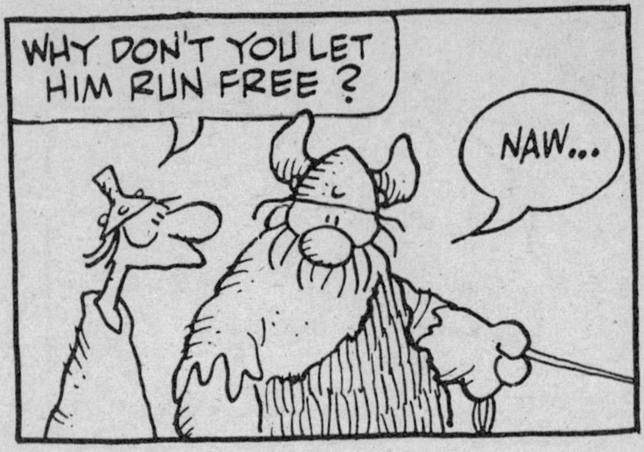
WHY DON'T YOU LET HIM RUN FREE ?
NAW...

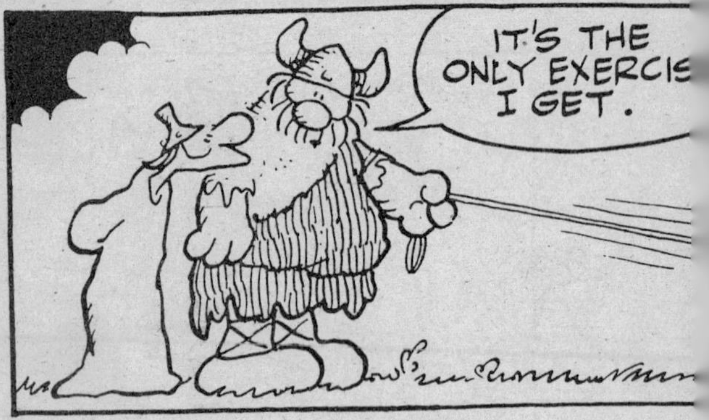
IT'S THE ONLY EXERCIS I GET .

LINGERONS!

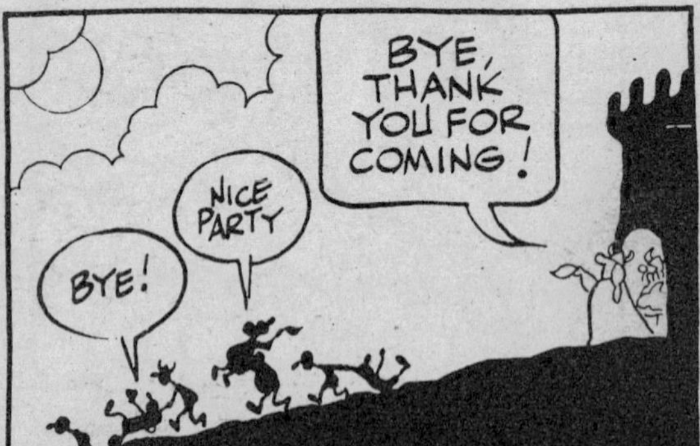
BYE!
NICE PARTY
BYE, THANK YOU FOR COMING !

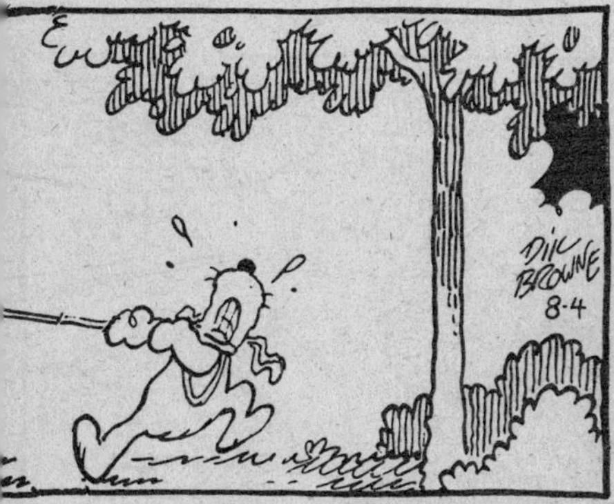
DIK BROWNE
8-4

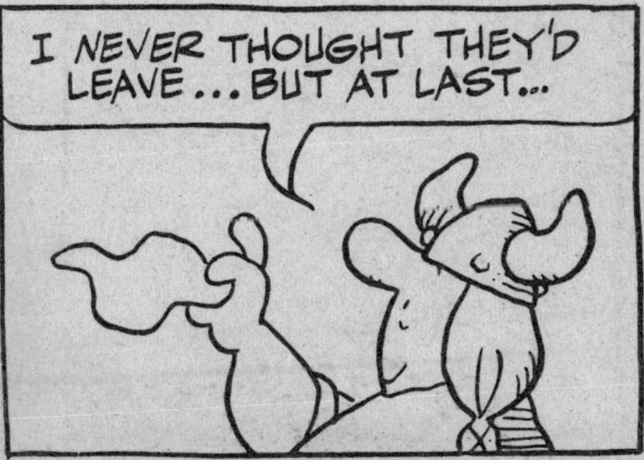
I NEVER THOUGHT THEY'D LEAVE... BUT AT LAST...

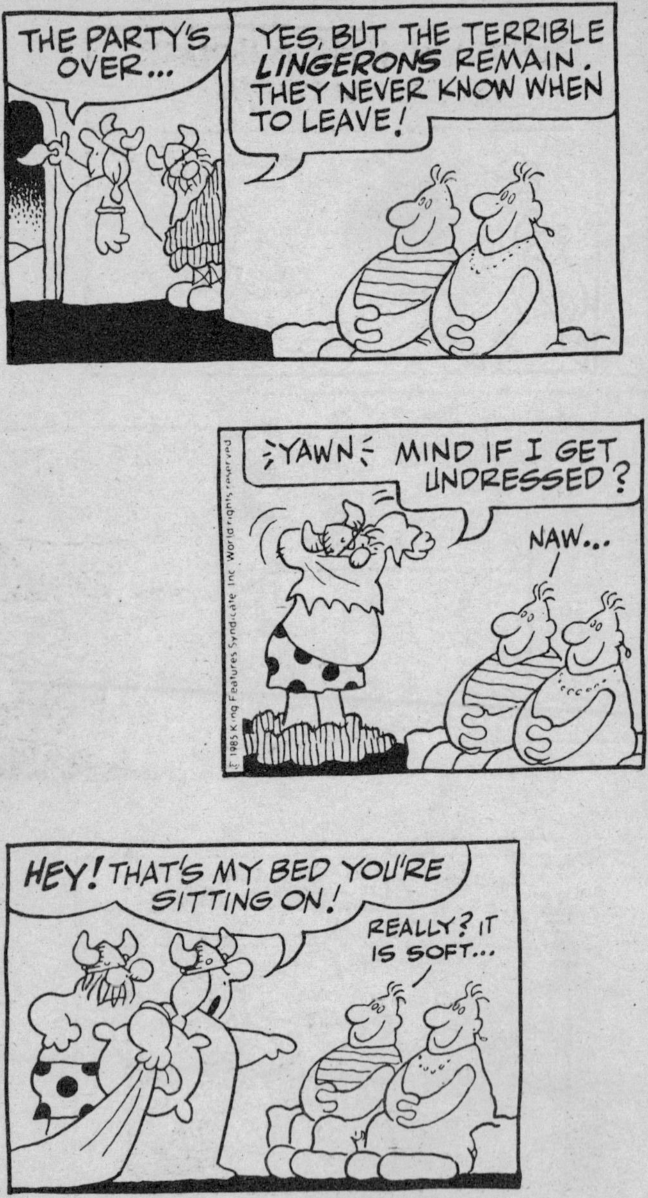
THE PARTY'S OVER...
YES, BUT THE TERRIBLE LINGERONS REMAIN. THEY NEVER KNOW WHEN TO LEAVE!
YAWN MIND IF I GET UNDRESSED?
NAW...
© 1985 King Features Syndicate Inc World rights reserved
HEY! THAT'S MY BED YOU'RE SITTING ON!
REALLY? IT IS SOFT...

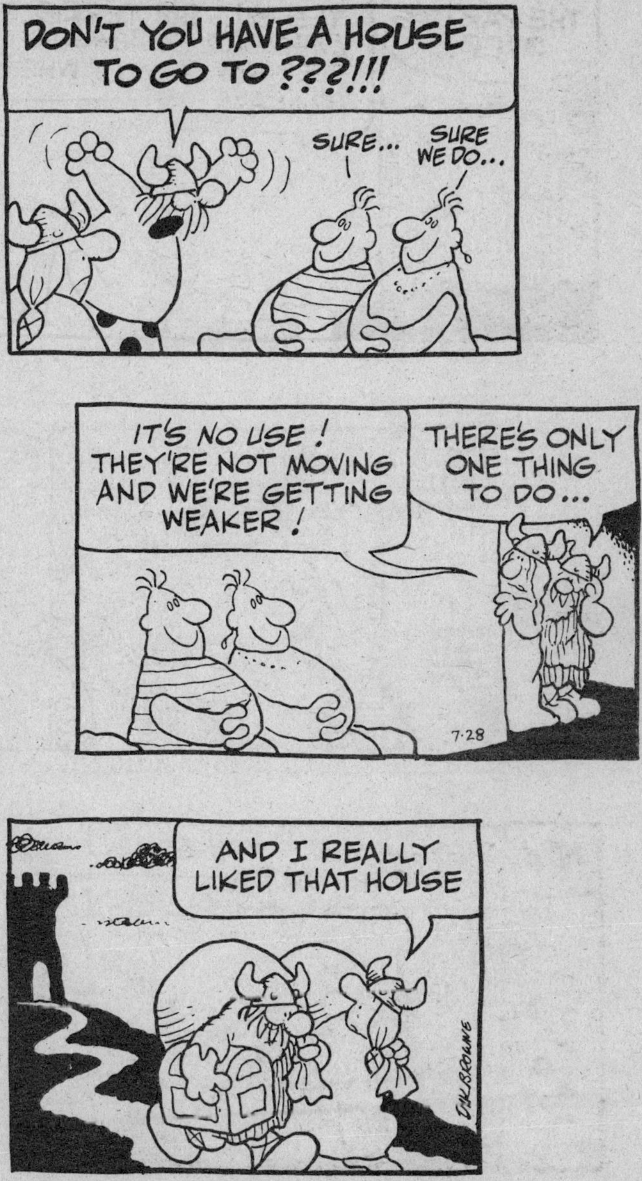
DON'T YOU HAVE A HOUSE TO GO TO ???!!!
SURE...
SURE WE DO...
IT'S NO USE! THEY'RE NOT MOVING AND WE'RE GETTING WEAKER!
THERE'S ONLY ONE THING TO DO...
7·28
AND I REALLY LIKED THAT HOUSE
DIK BROWNE

WHAT A WOMAN

HERE'S A CLEAN HANDKERCHIEF AND A NICE LUNCH—HAVE A NICE RAID ON ENGLAND
HEY! HAVEN'T YOU FORGOTTEN SOMETHING?
OH, YES!

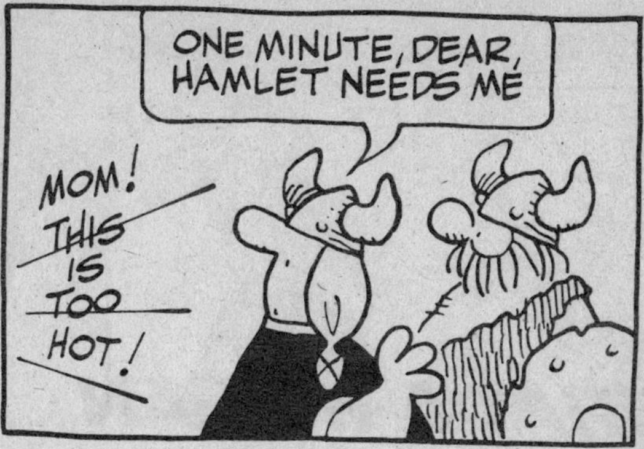
ONE MINUTE, DEAR, HAMLET NEEDS ME
MOM! THIS IS TOO HOT!

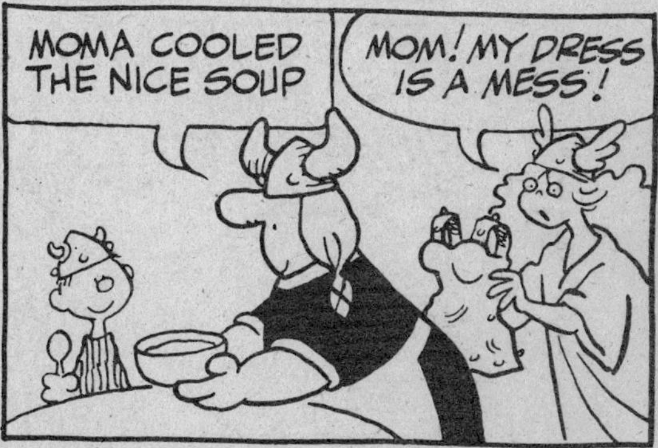
MOMA COOLED THE NICE SOUP
MOM! MY DRESS IS A MESS!

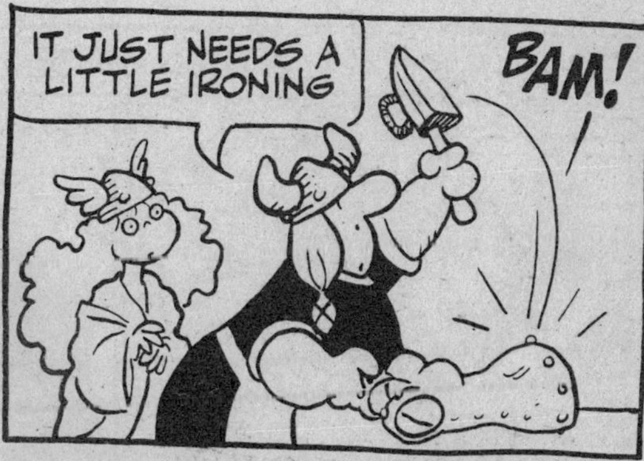
IT JUST NEEDS A LITTLE IRONING
BAM!

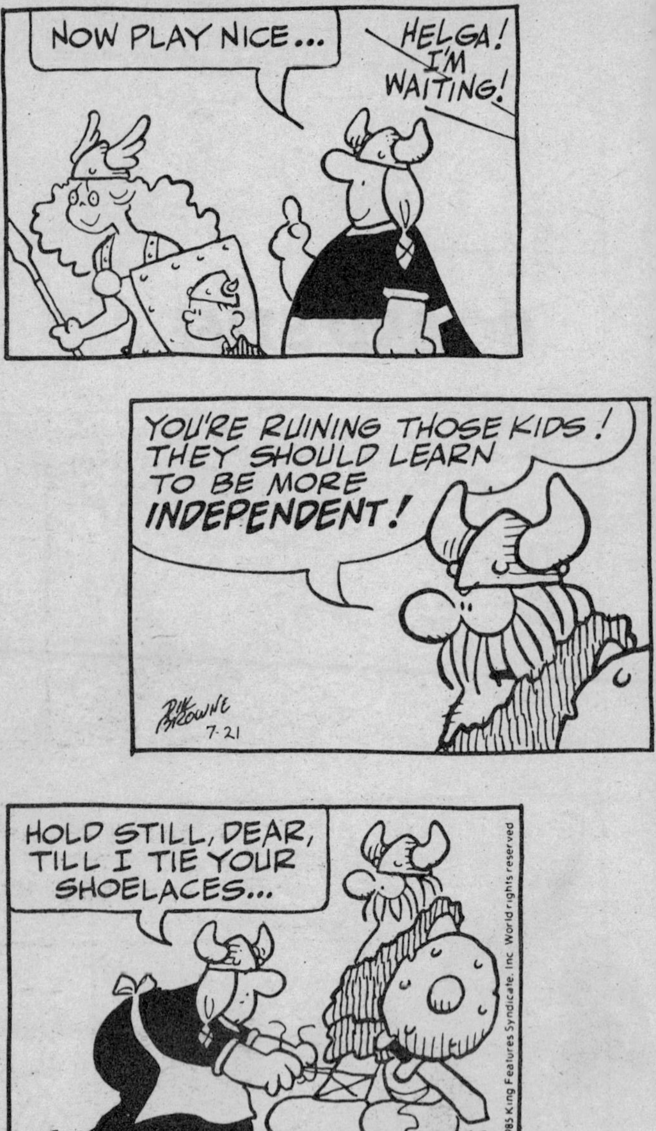
NOW PLAY NICE...
HELGA! I'M WAITING!
YOU'RE RUINING THOSE KIDS! THEY SHOULD LEARN TO BE MORE **INDEPENDENT**!
DIK BROWNE 7-21
HOLD STILL, DEAR, TILL I TIE YOUR SHOELACES...
© 1985 King Features Syndicate, Inc. World rights reserved

BOARD STIFF

EACH YEAR, WHEN THE SUMMER SUN SITS ATOP *THOR'S MOUNTAIN*...

BEHOLD!

EXCITEMENT SWEEPS THE LAND AND PEOPLE RUSH TO THE *PLACE WHERE THE DEED WILL BE DONE !*

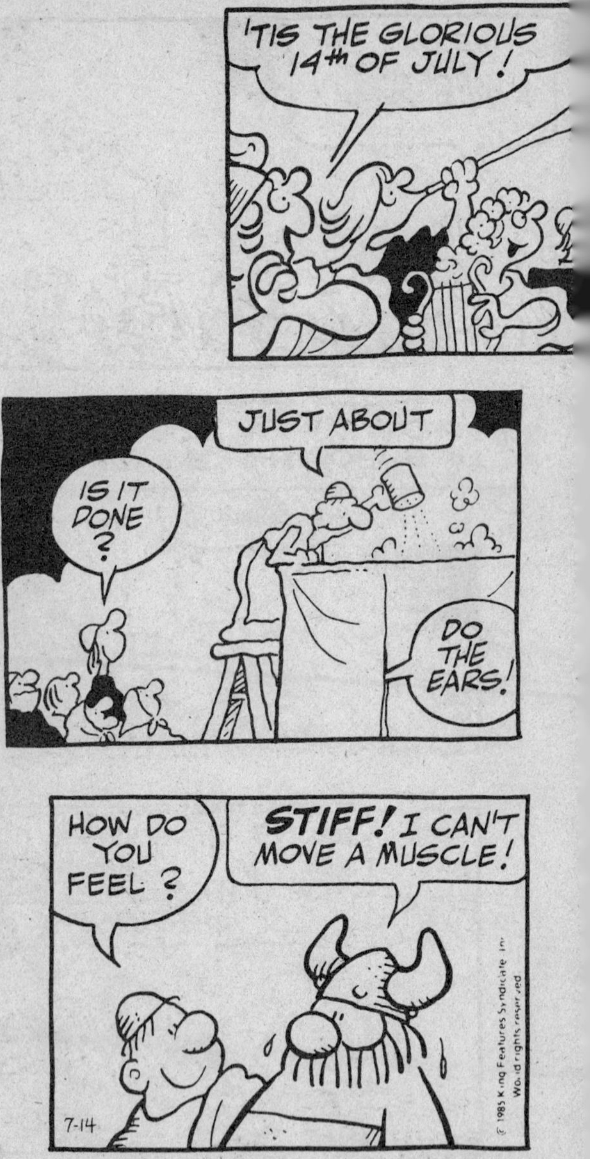
'TIS THE GLORIOUS 14th OF JULY!
JUST ABOUT
IS IT DONE ?
DO THE EARS!
HOW DO YOU FEEL ?
STIFF! I CAN'T MOVE A MUSCLE!
7-14
© 1985 King Features Syndicate Inc. World rights reserved.

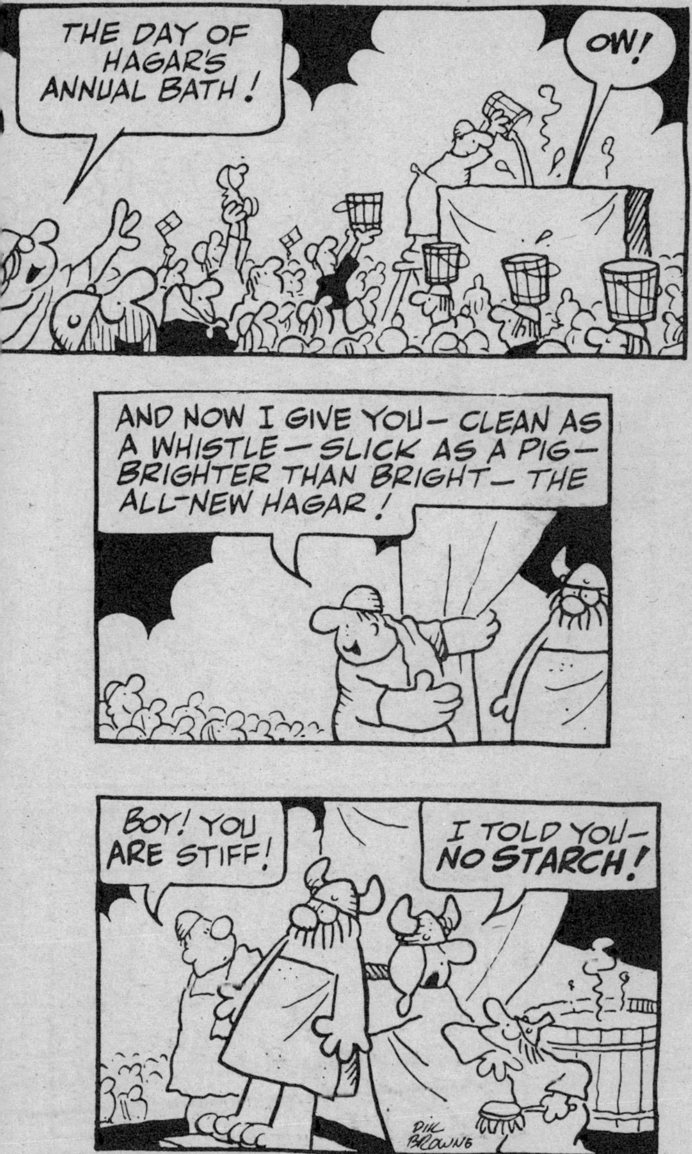
THE DAY OF HAGAR'S ANNUAL BATH!
OW!
AND NOW I GIVE YOU— CLEAN AS A WHISTLE— SLICK AS A PIG— BRIGHTER THAN BRIGHT— THE ALL-NEW HAGAR!
BOY! YOU ARE STIFF!
I TOLD YOU— NO STARCH!
DIK BROWNE

ALIEN

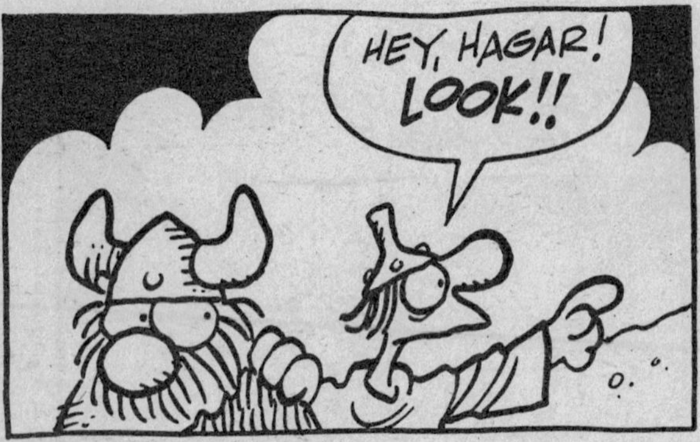
HEY, HAGAR! LOOK!!

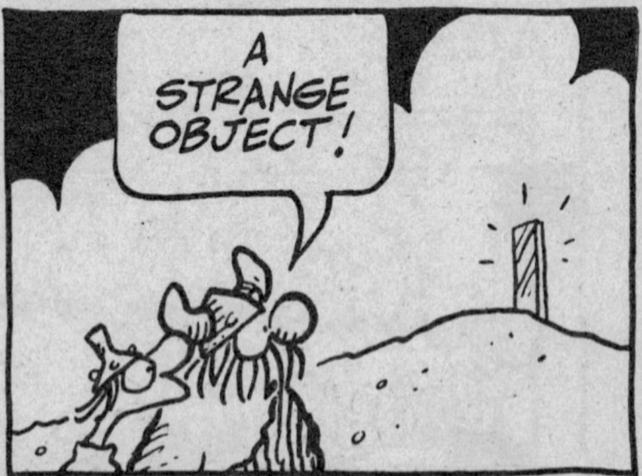
A STRANGE OBJECT!

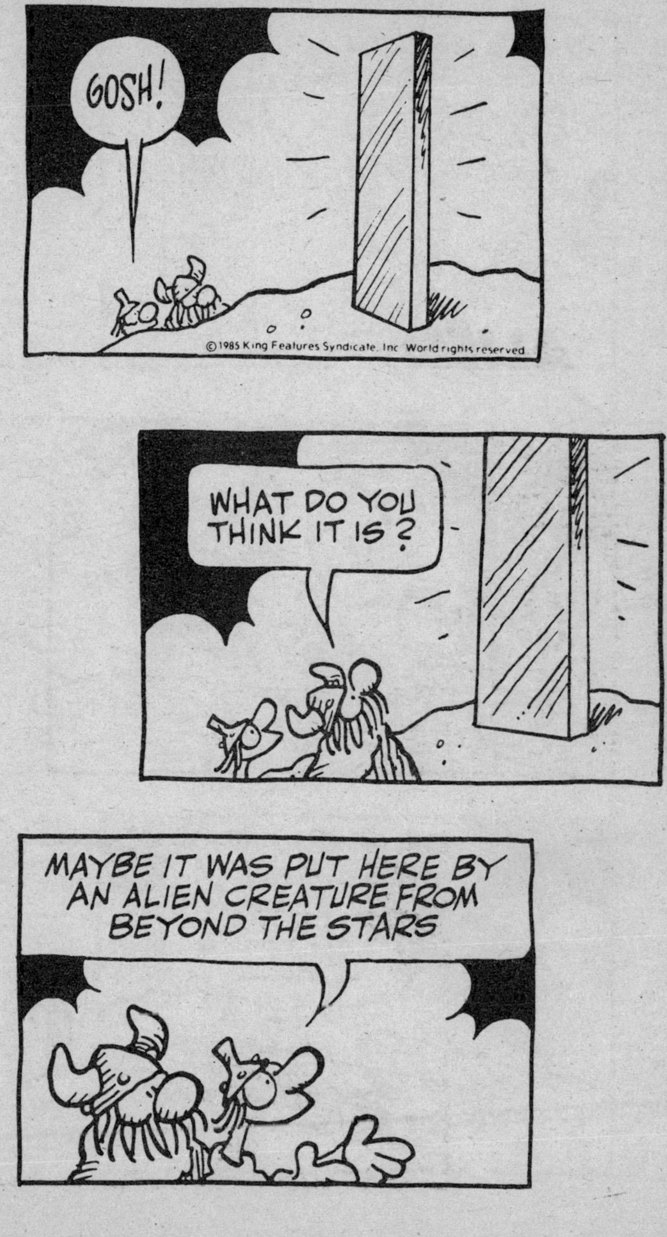
GOSH!
©1985 King Features Syndicate, Inc World rights reserved
WHAT DO YOU THINK IT IS?
MAYBE IT WAS PUT HERE BY AN ALIEN CREATURE FROM BEYOND THE STARS

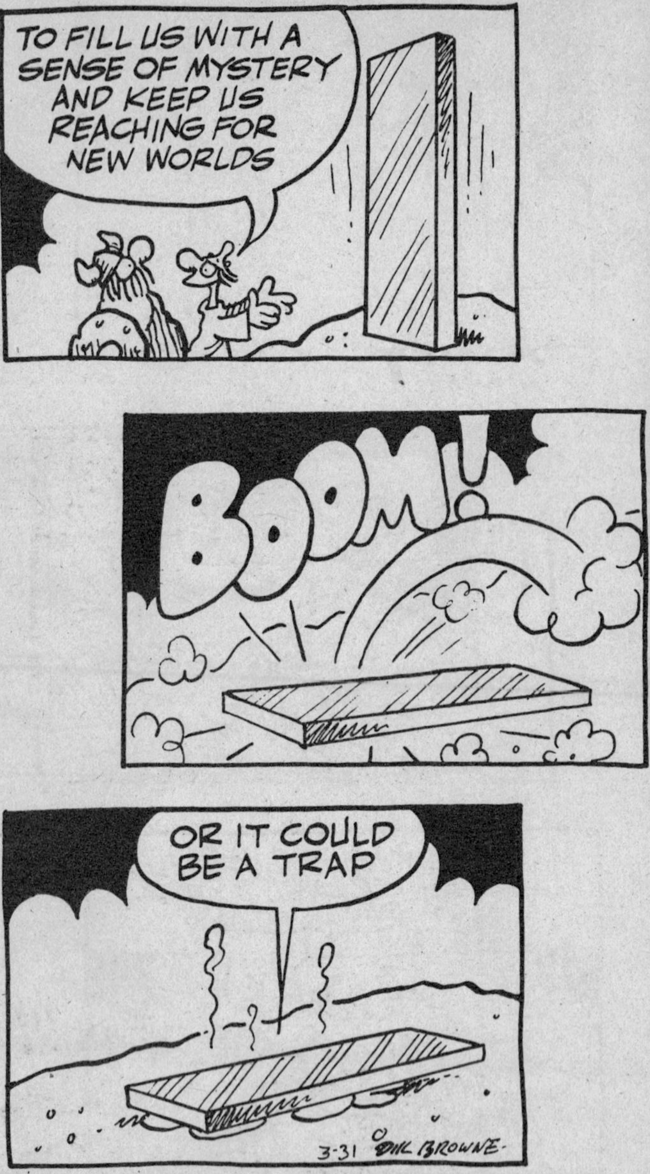
TO FILL US WITH A SENSE OF MYSTERY AND KEEP US REACHING FOR NEW WORLDS
BOOM!
OR IT COULD BE A TRAP
3-31 © DIK BROWNE

GUILT

I HEAR YOU! I HEAR YOU!
VOOF
VOOF
CAN'T YOU WAIT TILL I FINISH MY...
VOOF!!!

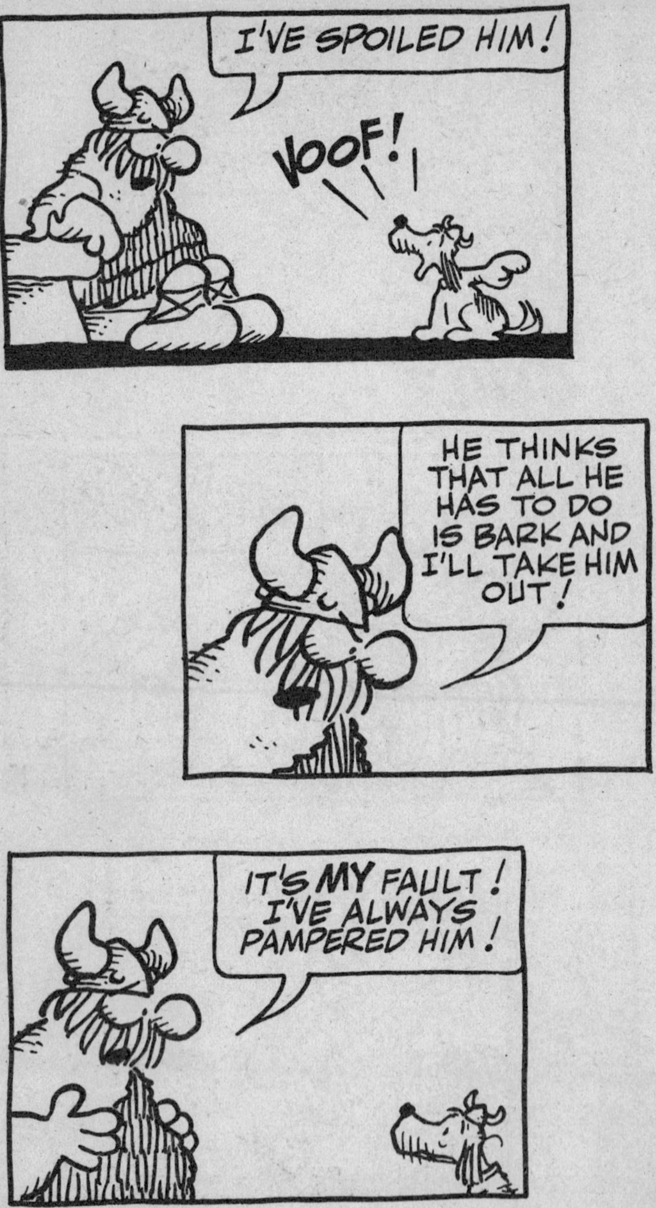
I'VE SPOILED HIM!
WOOF!
HE THINKS THAT ALL HE HAS TO DO IS BARK AND I'LL TAKE HIM OUT!
IT'S MY FAULT! I'VE ALWAYS PAMPERED HIM!

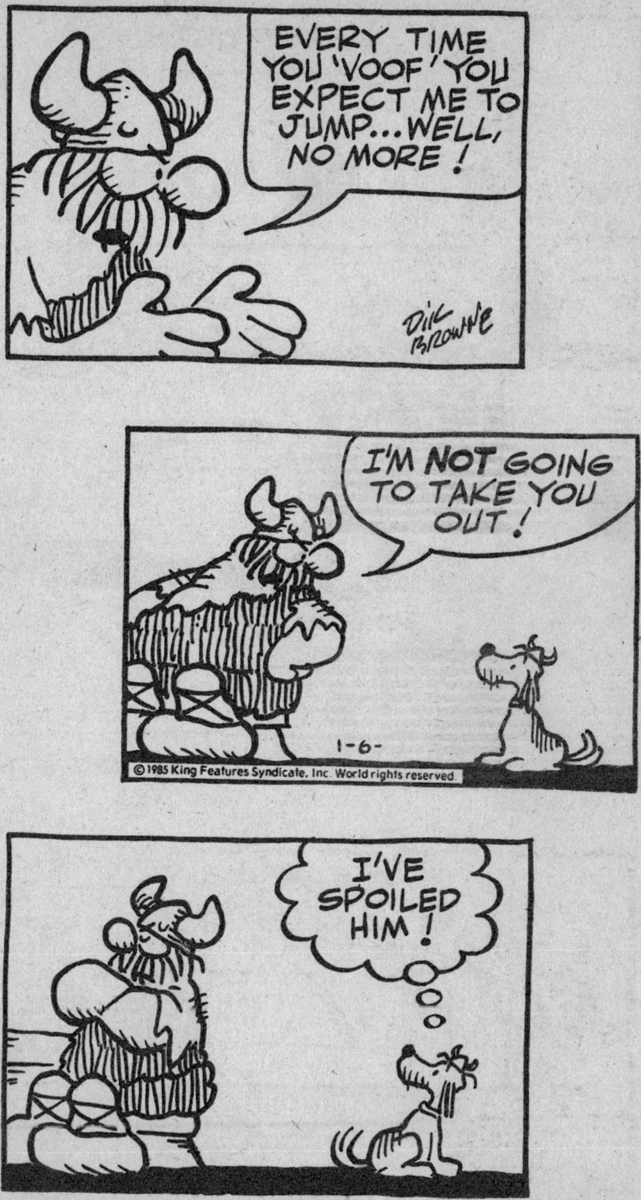
EVERY TIME YOU 'VOOF' YOU EXPECT ME TO JUMP...WELL, NO MORE!
DIK BROWNE
I'M **NOT** GOING TO TAKE YOU OUT!
1-6-
© 1985 King Features Syndicate, Inc. World rights reserved.
I'VE SPOILED HIM!

NUF DU POP!

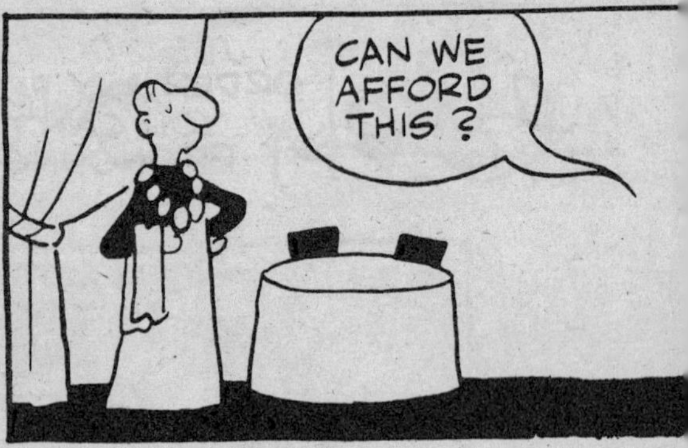
CAN WE AFFORD THIS ?

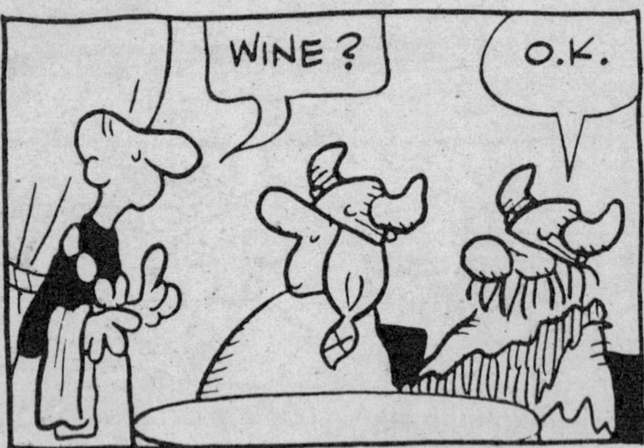
WINE ?
O.K.

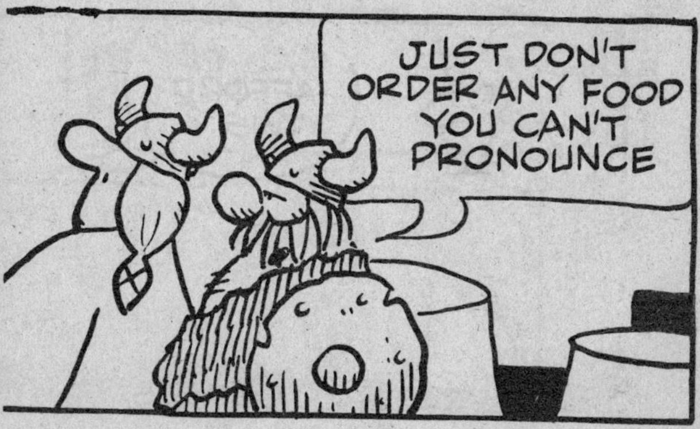
JUST DON'T ORDER ANY FOOD YOU CAN'T PRONOUNCE

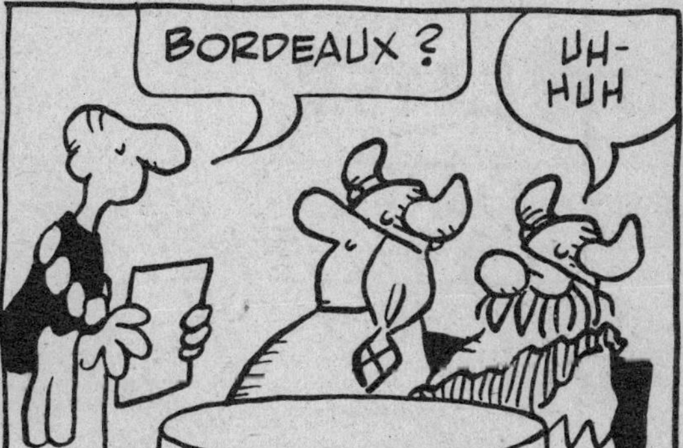
BORDEAUX ?
UH-HUH

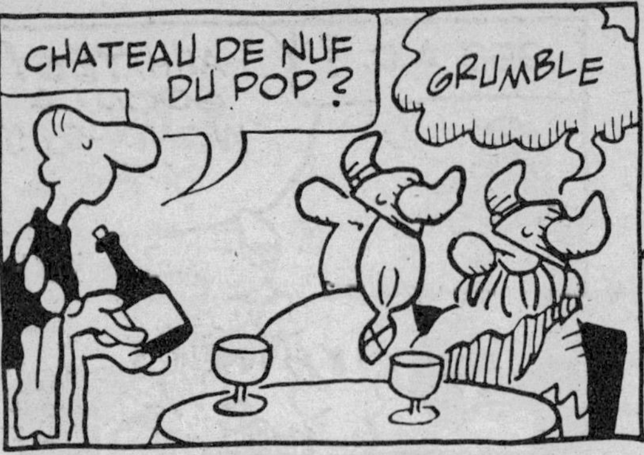

CHATEAU DE NUF DU POP?
GRUMBLE

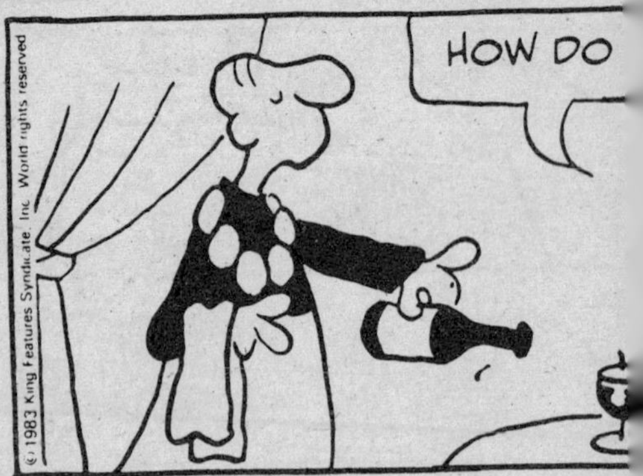

HOW DO
© 1983 King Features Syndicate, Inc. World rights reserved

SLOW EATER

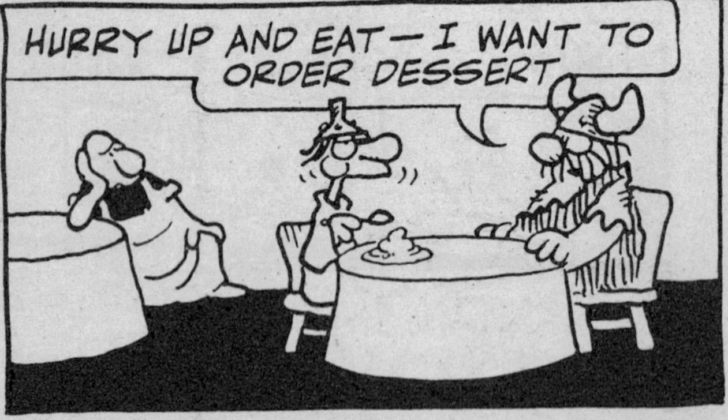

HURRY UP AND EAT—I WANT TO ORDER DESSERT

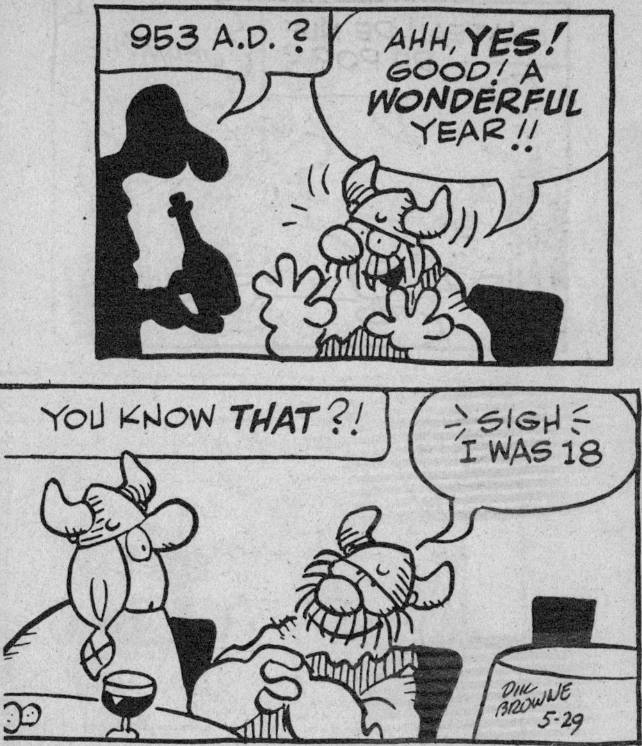
953 A.D.?
AHH, YES! GOOD! A WONDERFUL YEAR!!
YOU KNOW THAT?!
SIGH
I WAS 18
DIK BROWNE 5-29

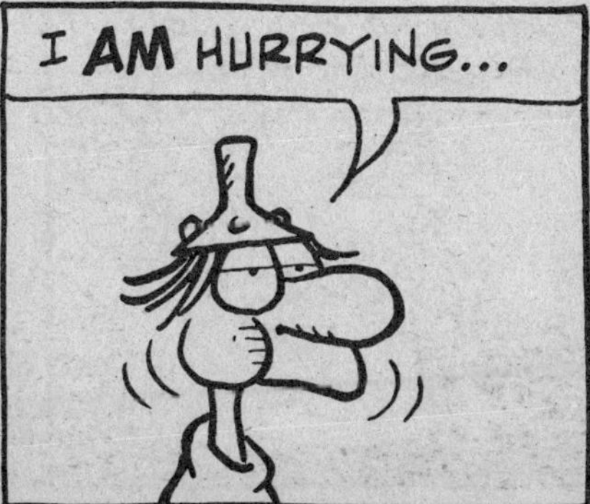
I AM HURRYING...

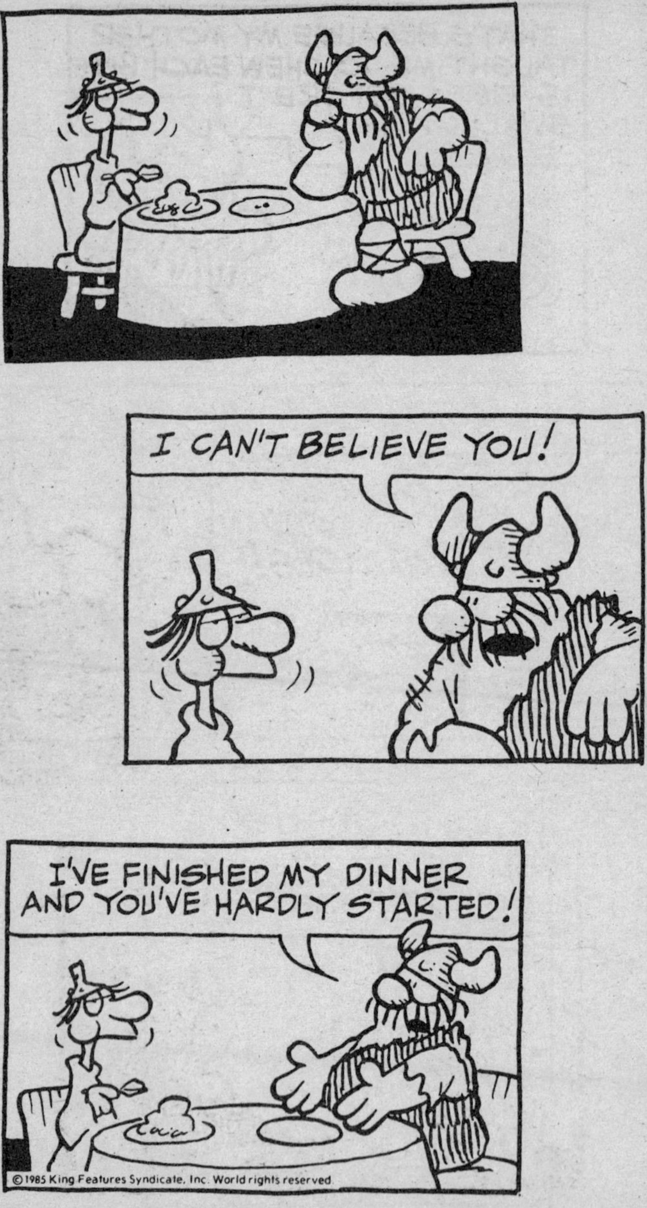
I CAN'T BELIEVE YOU!
I'VE FINISHED MY DINNER AND YOU'VE HARDLY STARTED!

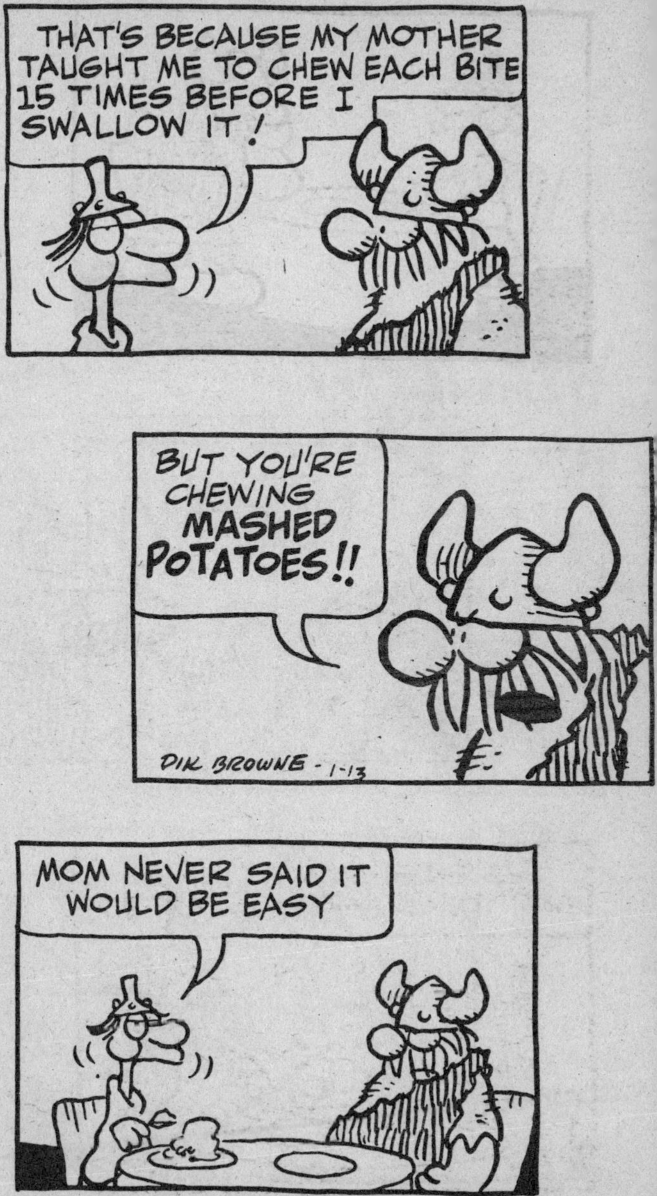
THAT'S BECAUSE MY MOTHER TAUGHT ME TO CHEW EACH BITE 15 TIMES BEFORE I SWALLOW IT!
BUT YOU'RE CHEWING MASHED POTATOES!!
DIK BROWNE - 1-13
MOM NEVER SAID IT WOULD BE EASY

STANDOFF

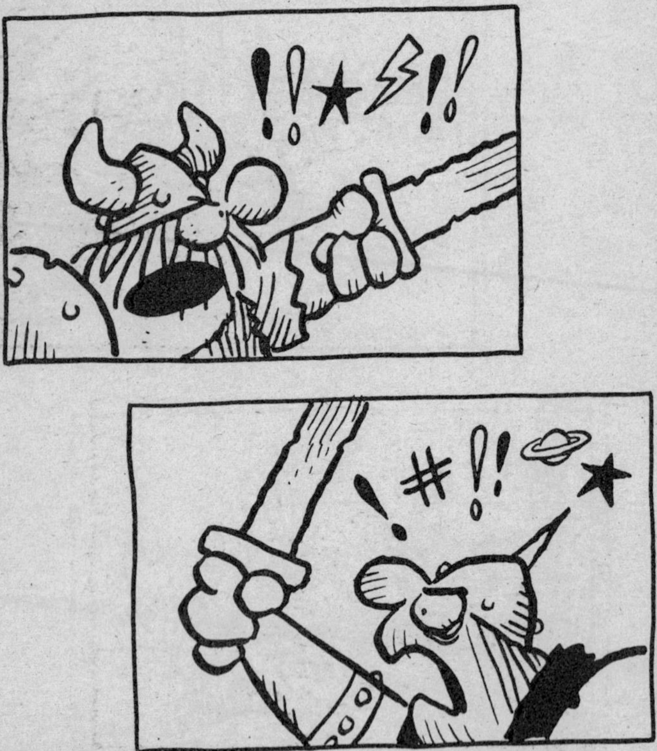

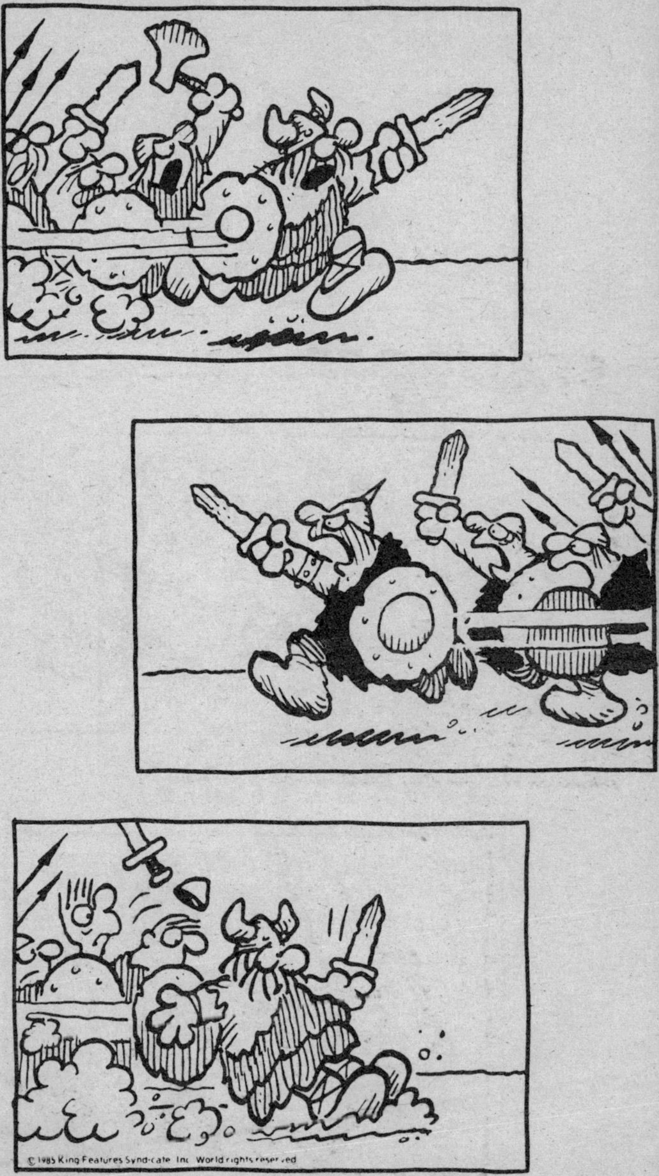
© 1985 King Features Syndicate, Inc. World rights reserved

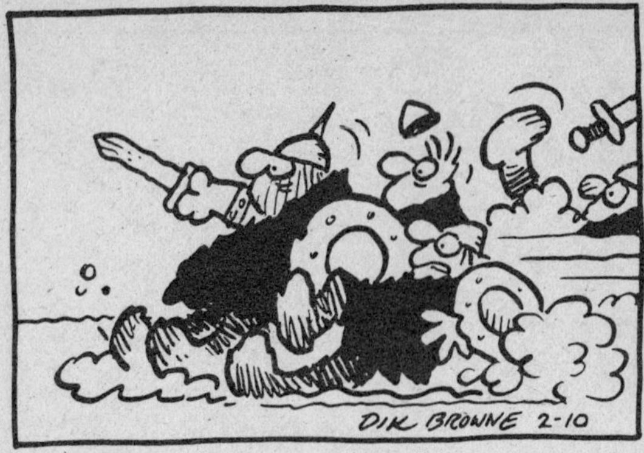
DIK BROWNE 2-10

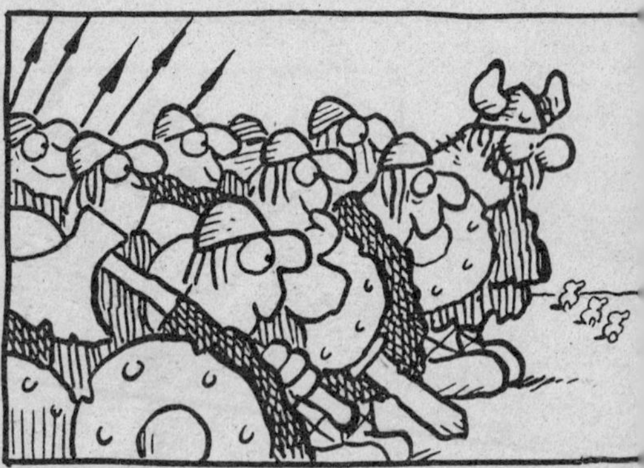

INSPECTION

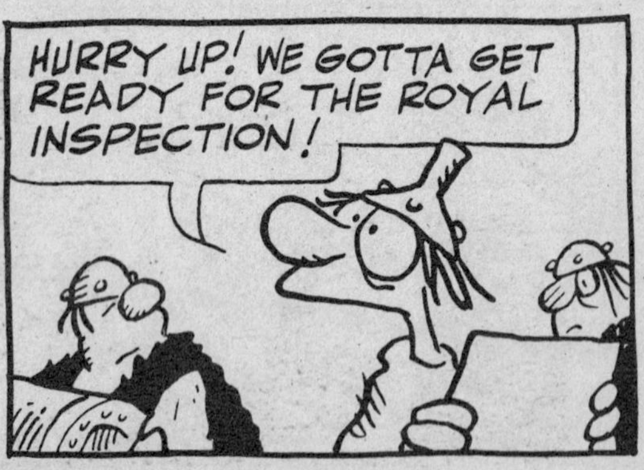
HURRY UP! WE GOTTA GET READY FOR THE ROYAL INSPECTION!

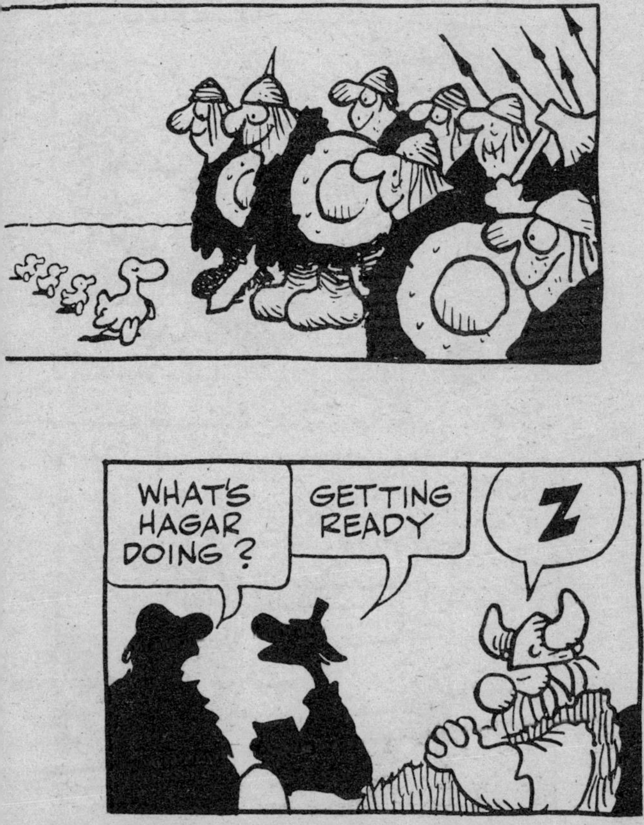
WHAT'S HAGAR DOING?
GETTING READY
Z

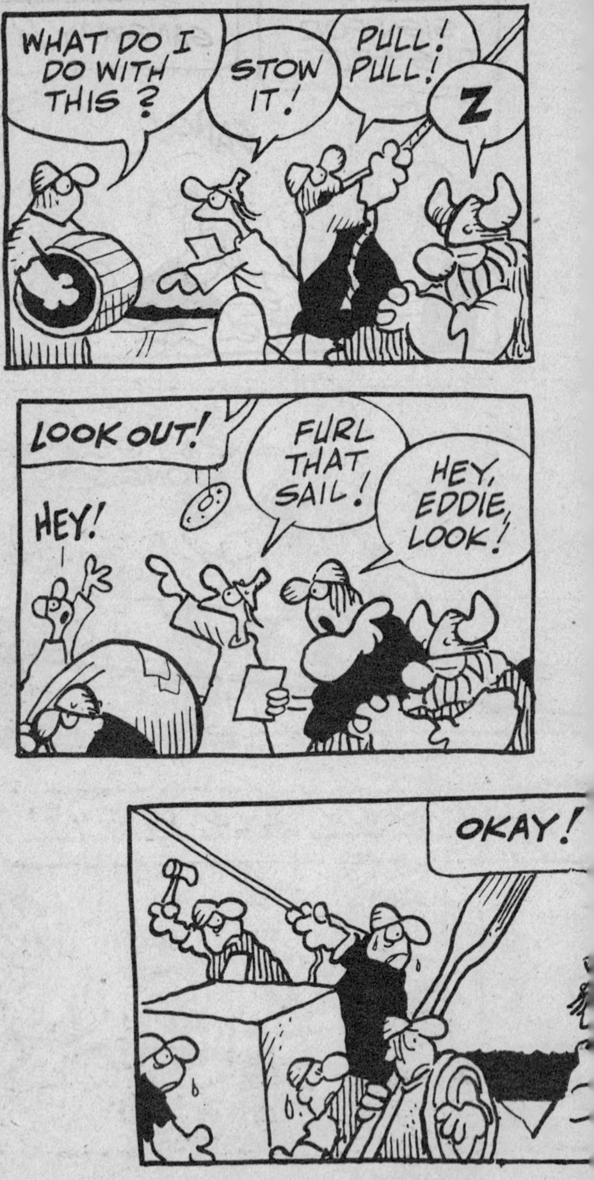
WHAT DO I DO WITH THIS?
STOW IT!
PULL! PULL!
Z
LOOK OUT!
HEY!
FURL THAT SAIL!
HEY, EDDIE, LOOK!
OKAY!

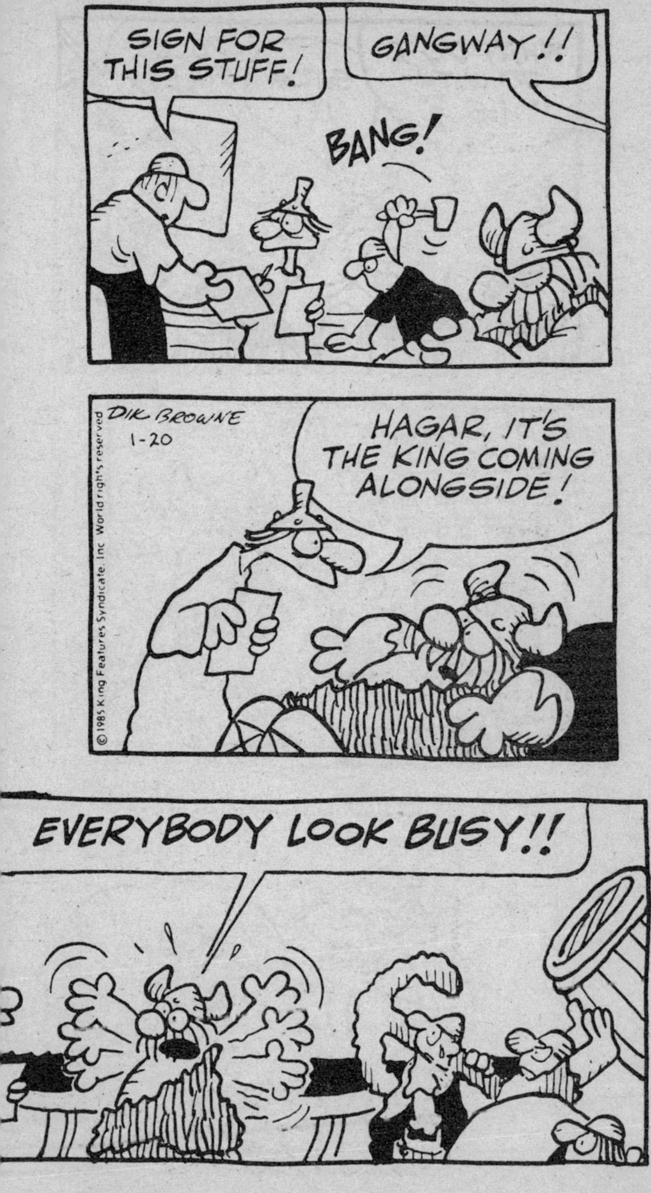

SIGN FOR THIS STUFF!
GANGWAY!!
BANG!
DIK BROWNE
1-20
© 1985 King Features Syndicate, Inc World righ's reserved
HAGAR, IT'S THE KING COMING ALONGSIDE!
EVERYBODY LOOK BUSY!!

NOT SATISFIED

SNERT! STOP THAT! YOU KNOW I HATE WHINING AND BEGGING!
...HELGA?

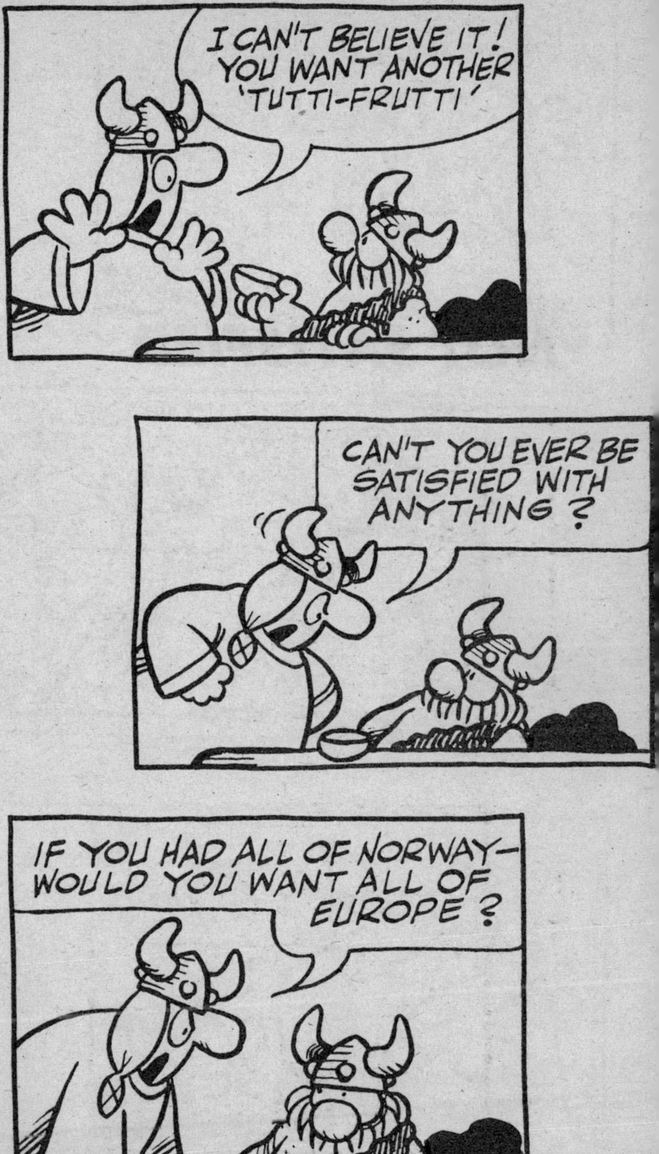
I CAN'T BELIEVE IT! YOU WANT ANOTHER 'TUTTI-FRUTTI'
CAN'T YOU EVER BE SATISFIED WITH ANYTHING ?
IF YOU HAD ALL OF NORWAY- WOULD YOU WANT ALL OF EUROPE ?

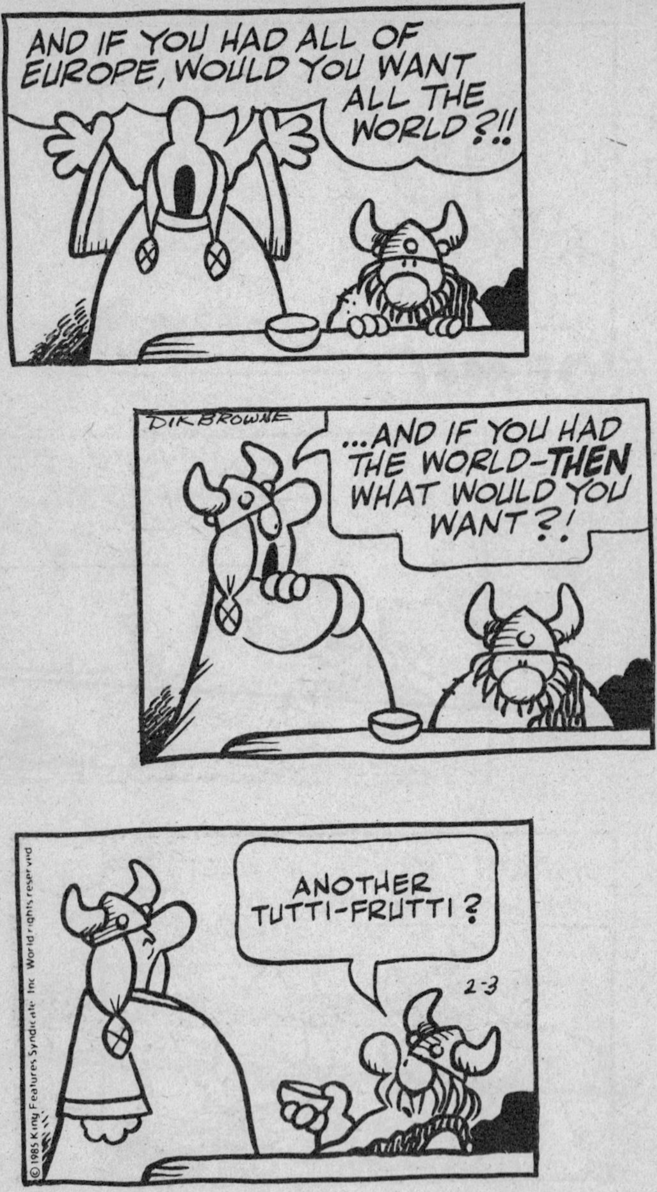
AND IF YOU HAD ALL OF EUROPE, WOULD YOU WANT ALL THE WORLD?!!
DIK BROWNE
...AND IF YOU HAD THE WORLD-**THEN** WHAT WOULD YOU WANT?!
ANOTHER TUTTI-FRUTTI?
2-3
© 1985 King Features Syndicate Inc World rights reserved

NOT ME!

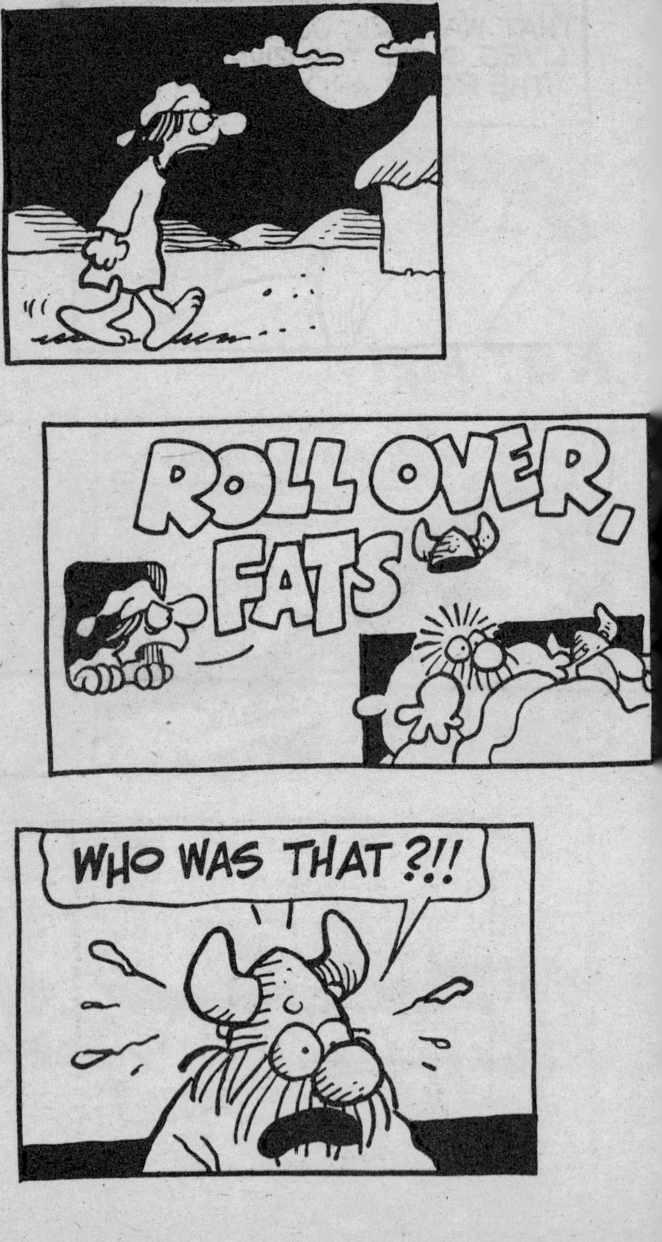
ROLL OVER, FATS
WHO WAS THAT ?!!

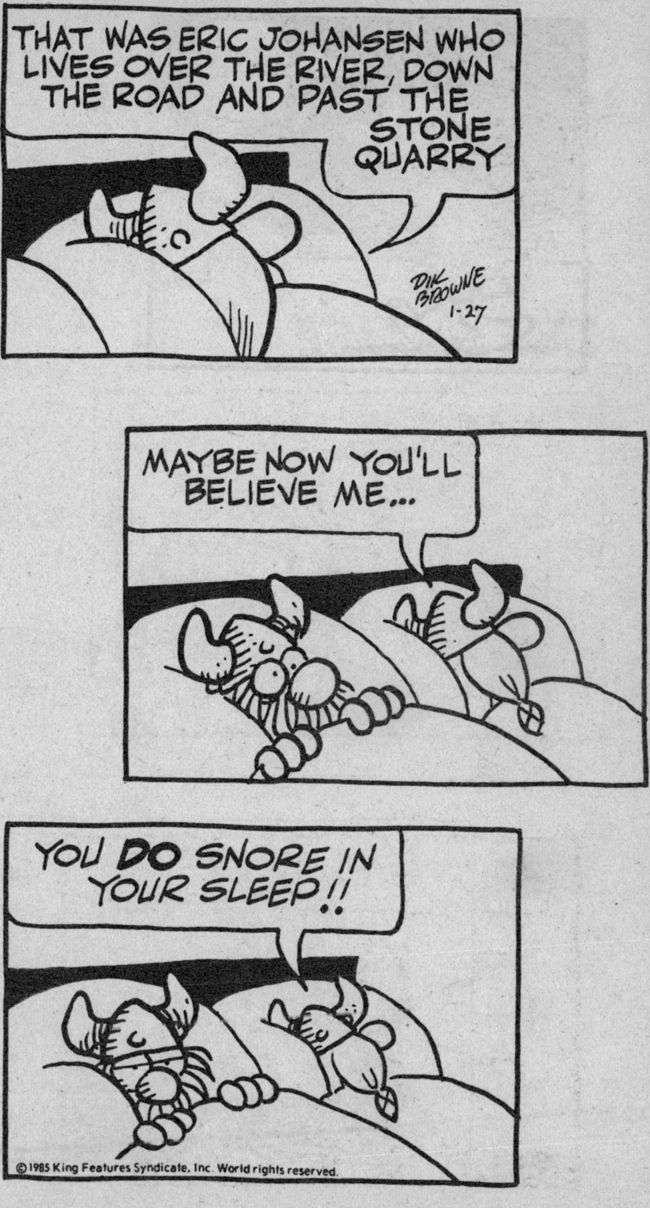
THAT WAS ERIC JOHANSEN WHO LIVES OVER THE RIVER, DOWN THE ROAD AND PAST THE STONE QUARRY
DIK BROWNE
1-27
MAYBE NOW YOU'LL BELIEVE ME...
YOU DO SNORE IN YOUR SLEEP!!

THE SAUCE

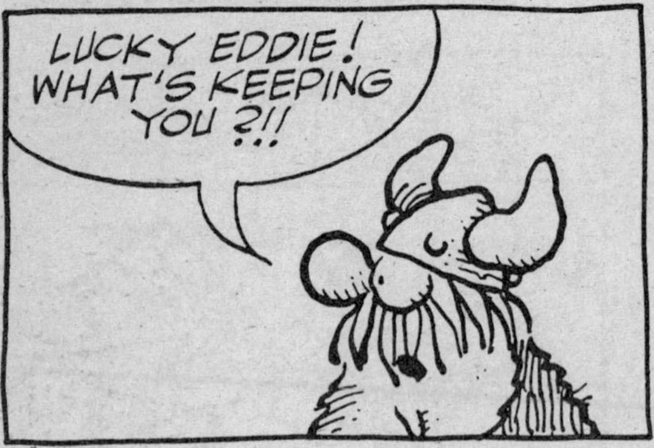
LUCKY EDDIE! WHAT'S KEEPING YOU ?!!

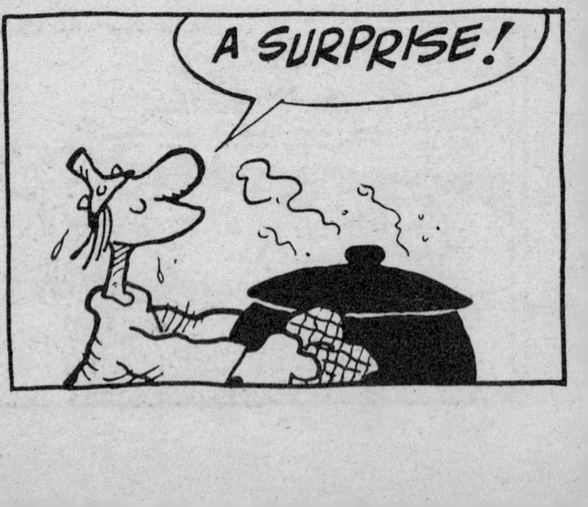
A SURPRISE!

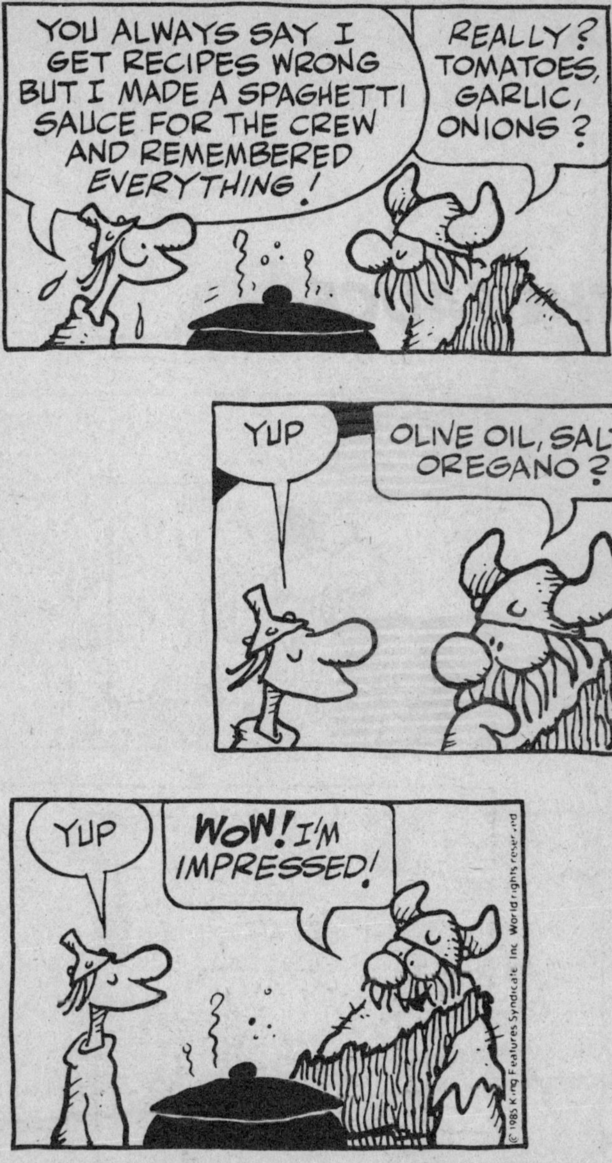

YOU ALWAYS SAY I GET RECIPES WRONG BUT I MADE A SPAGHETTI SAUCE FOR THE CREW AND REMEMBERED EVERYTHING!
REALLY? TOMATOES, GARLIC, ONIONS?
YUP
OLIVE OIL, SALT, OREGANO?
YUP
WOW! I'M IMPRESSED!
© 1985 King Features Syndicate Inc World rights reserved

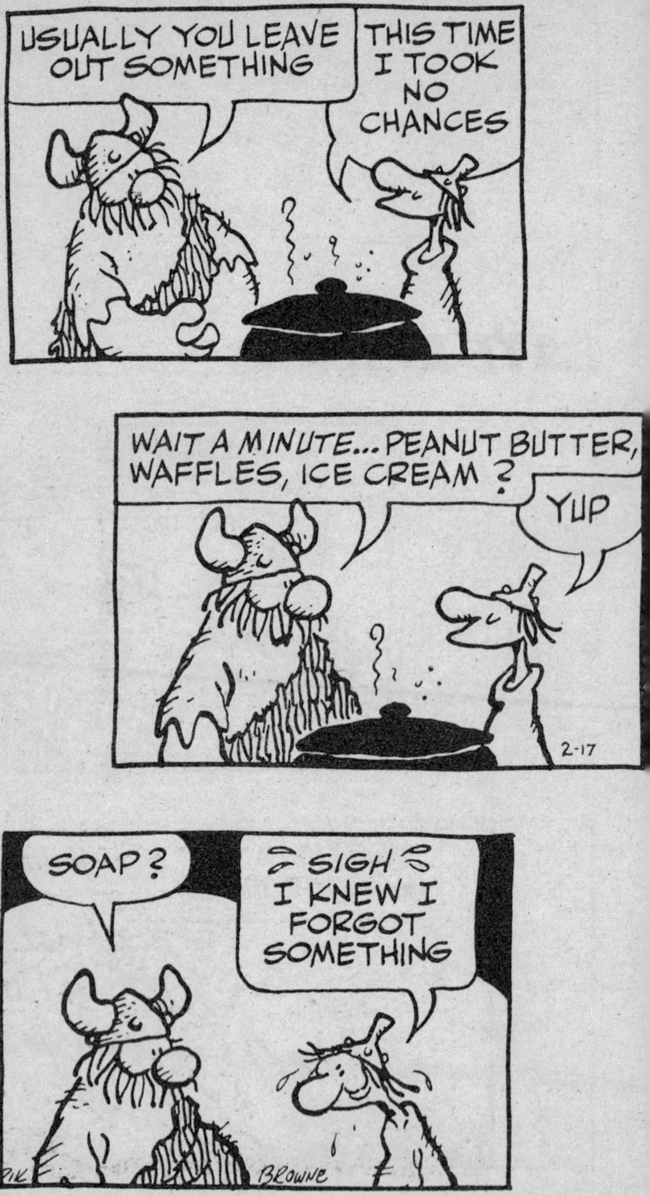
USUALLY YOU LEAVE OUT SOMETHING
THIS TIME I TOOK NO CHANCES
WAIT A MINUTE... PEANUT BUTTER, WAFFLES, ICE CREAM ?
YUP
2-17
SOAP ?
SIGH
I KNEW I FORGOT SOMETHING
BROWNE

LATE RISER

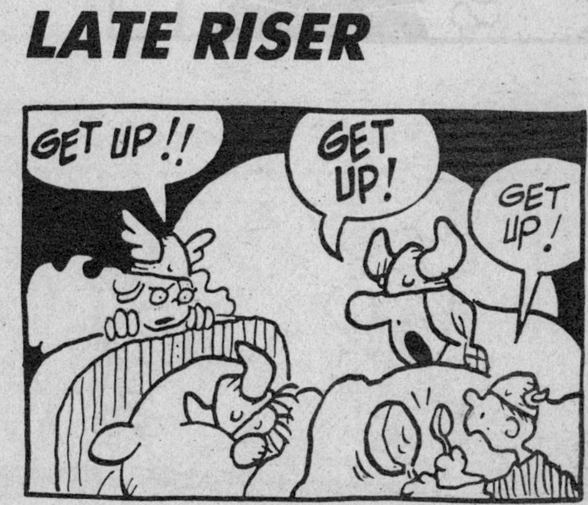
GET UP!!
GET UP!
GET UP!

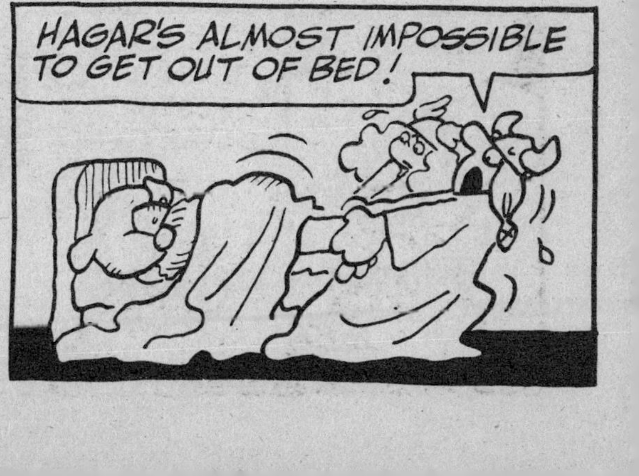
HAGAR'S ALMOST IMPOSSIBLE TO GET OUT OF BED!

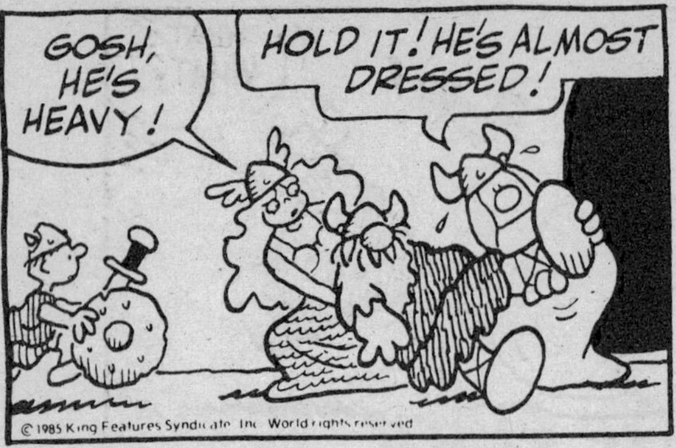
GOSH, HE'S HEAVY!
HOLD IT! HE'S ALMOST DRESSED!
© 1985 King Features Syndicate, Inc. World rights reserved

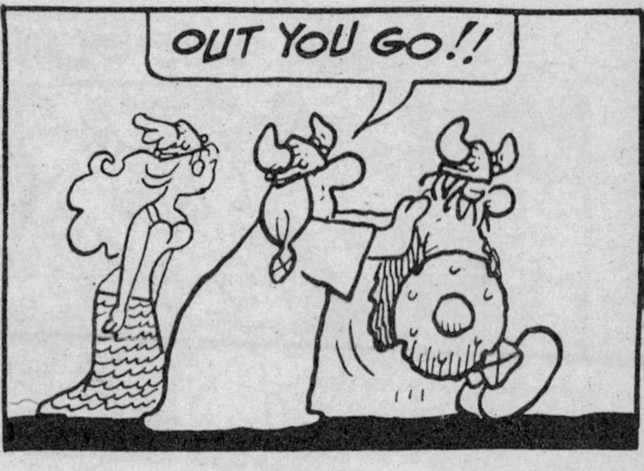
OUT YOU GO!!

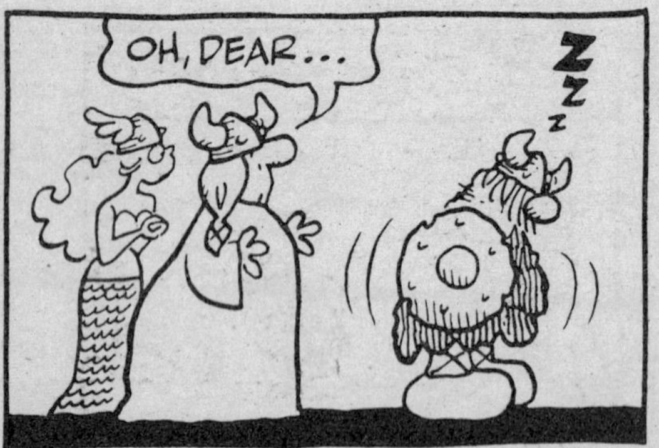
OH, DEAR...
Z Z z

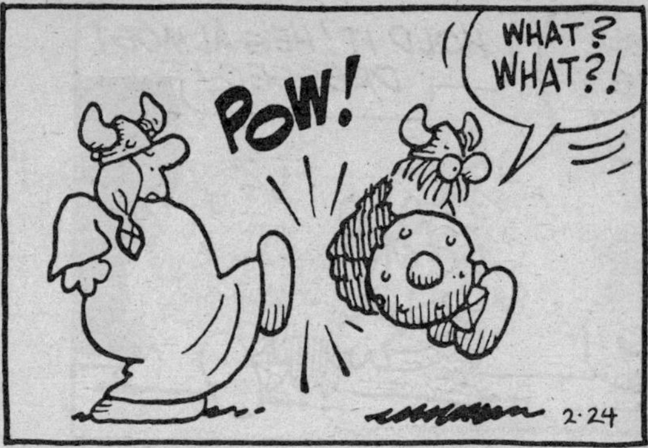
POW!
WHAT? WHAT?!
2·24

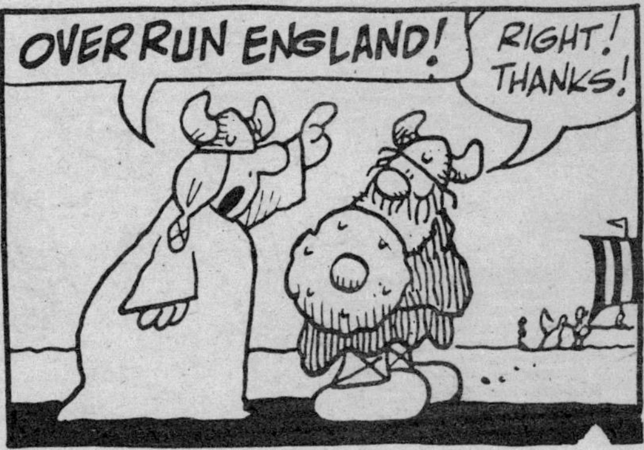
OVERRUN ENGLAND!
RIGHT! THANKS!

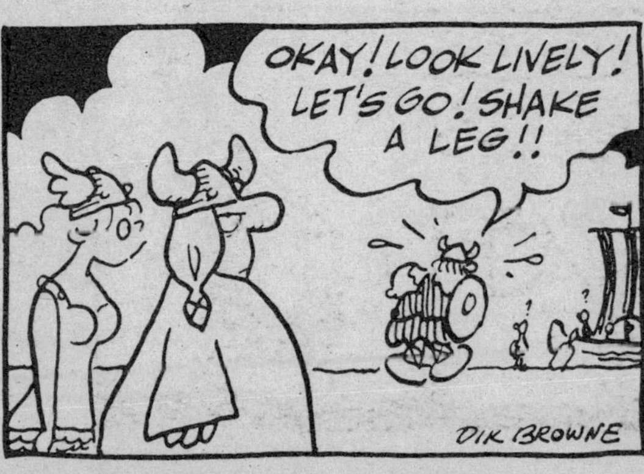
OKAY! LOOK LIVELY! LET'S GO! SHAKE A LEG!!
DIK BROWNE

TOO SHY

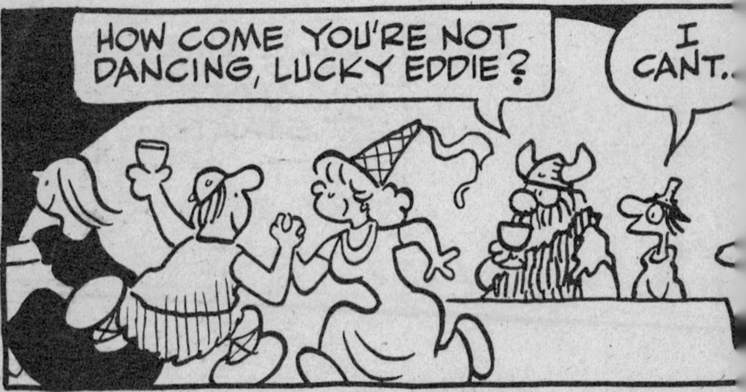
HOW COME YOU'RE NOT DANCING, LUCKY EDDIE?
I CANT..

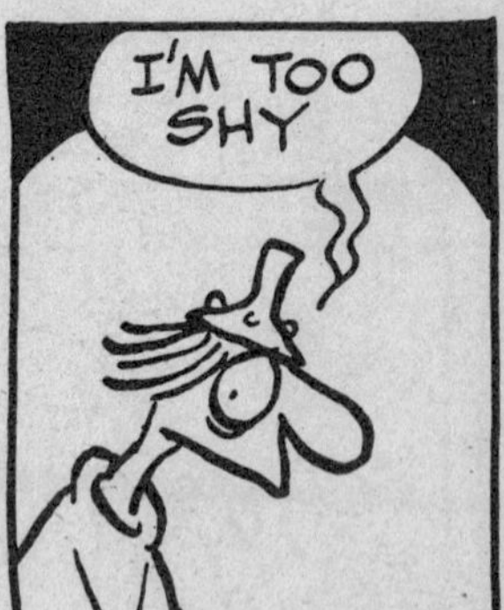
I'M TOO SHY

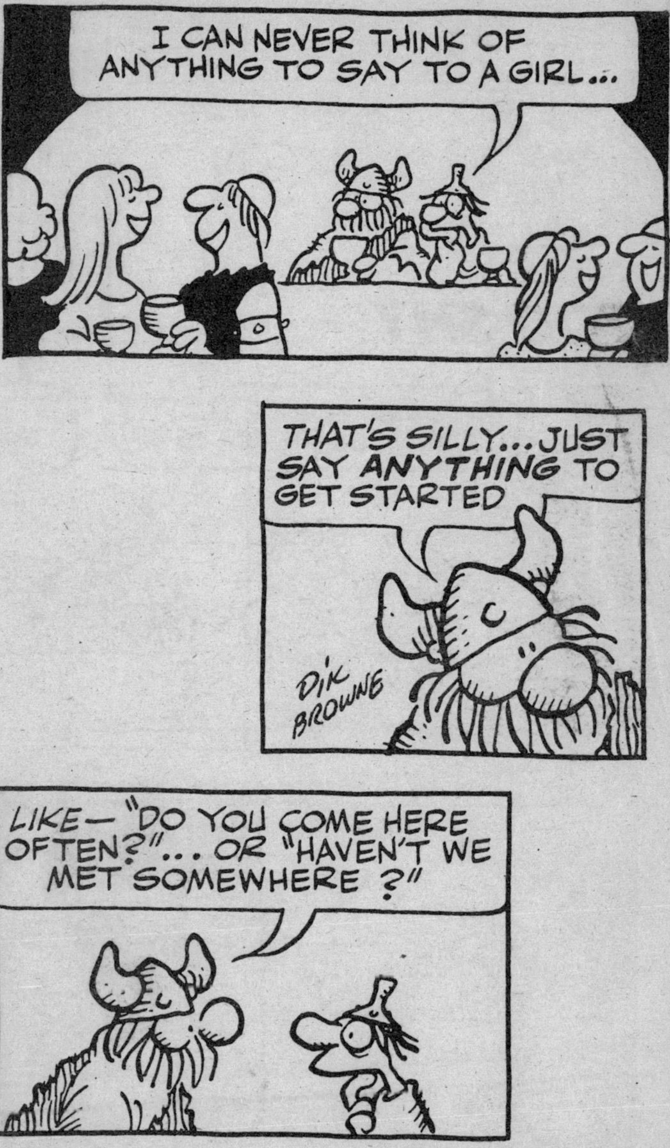
I CAN NEVER THINK OF ANYTHING TO SAY TO A GIRL...
THAT'S SILLY...JUST SAY ANYTHING TO GET STARTED
DIK BROWNE
LIKE— "DO YOU COME HERE OFTEN?"... OR "HAVEN'T WE MET SOMEWHERE ?"

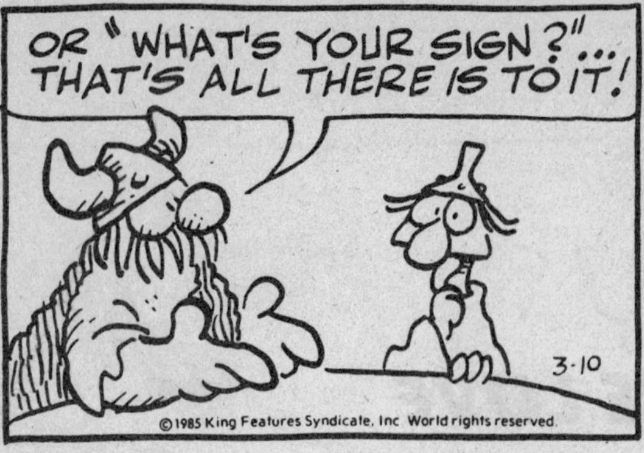
OR "WHAT'S YOUR SIGN?"... THAT'S ALL THERE IS TO IT!
3-10
©1985 King Features Syndicate, Inc World rights reserved.

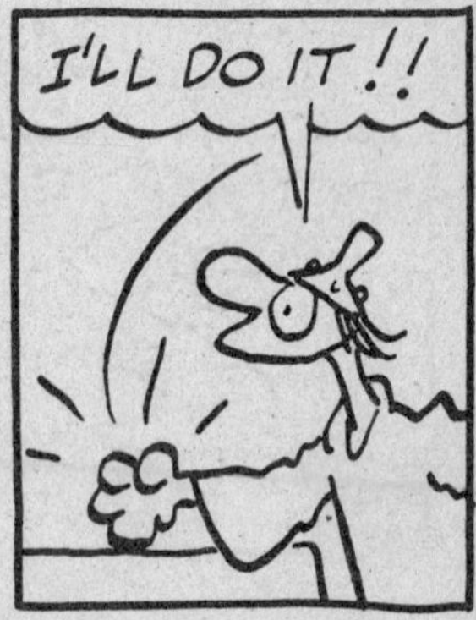
I'LL DO IT!!

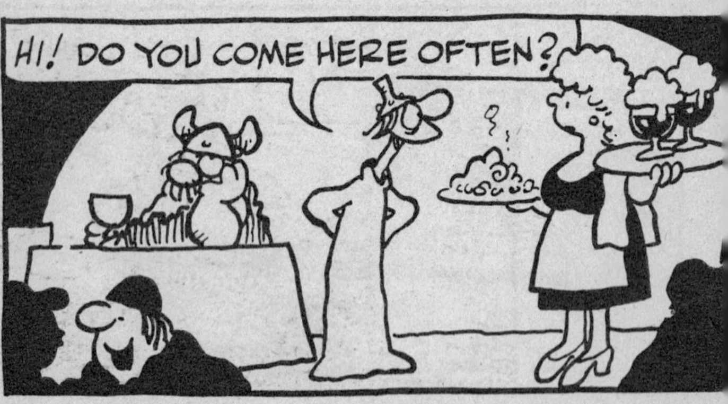
HI! DO YOU COME HERE OFTEN?

TRUE LOVE

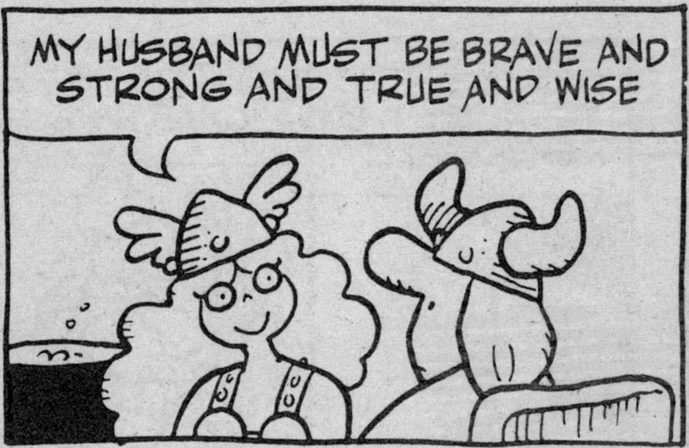
MY HUSBAND MUST BE BRAVE AND STRONG AND TRUE AND WISE

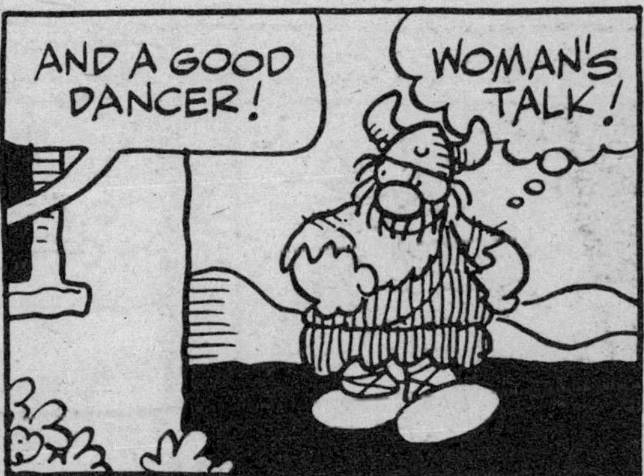
AND A GOOD DANCER!
WOMAN'S TALK!

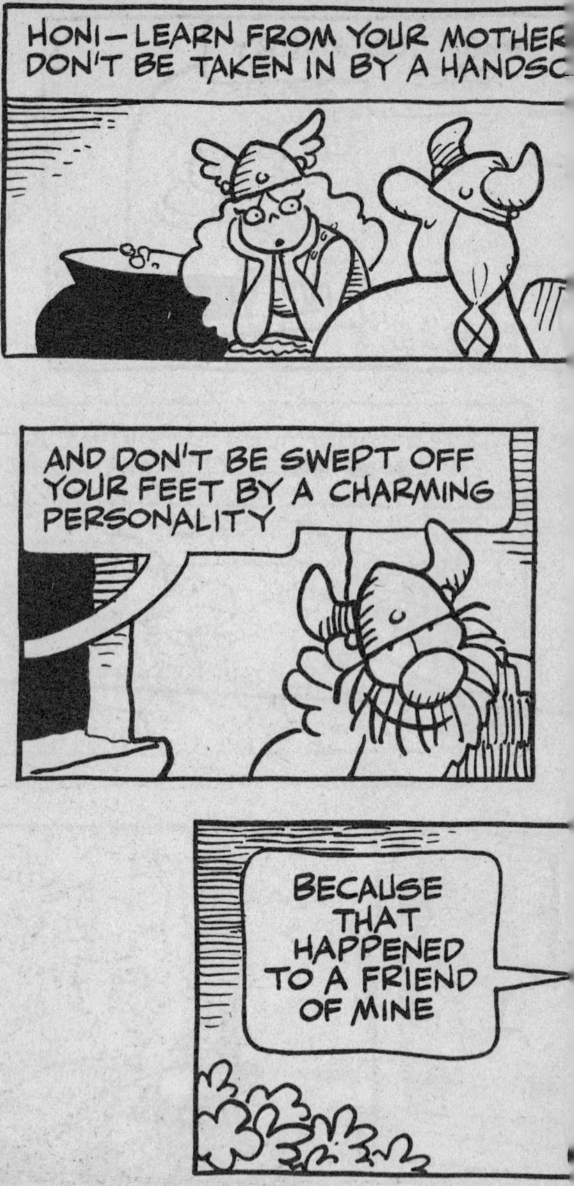
HONI—LEARN FROM YOUR MOTHER
DON'T BE TAKEN IN BY A HANDSO
AND DON'T BE SWEPT OFF YOUR FEET BY A CHARMING PERSONALITY
BECAUSE THAT HAPPENED TO A FRIEND OF MINE

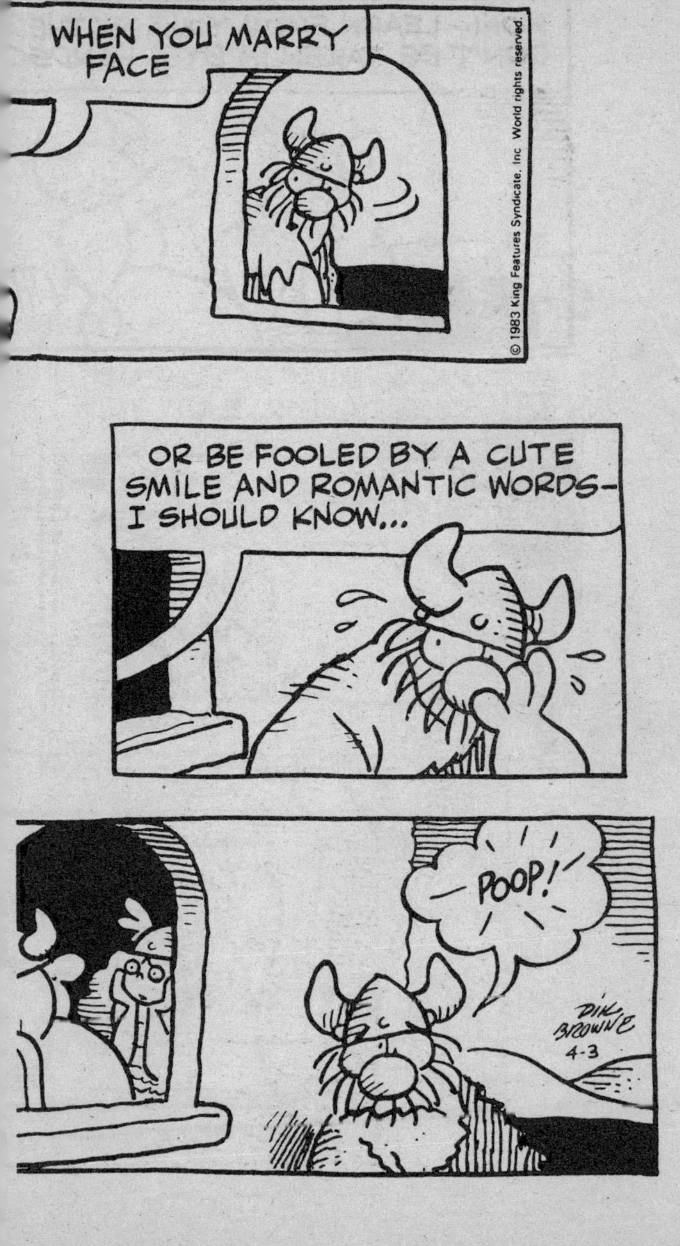
WHEN YOU MARRY FACE
© 1983 King Features Syndicate, Inc. World rights reserved.
OR BE FOOLED BY A CUTE SMILE AND ROMANTIC WORDS- I SHOULD KNOW...
POOP!
DIK BROWNE 4-3

CHARM

A VIKING MUST BE VIGILANT, FAITHFUL, BRAVE AND TRUE

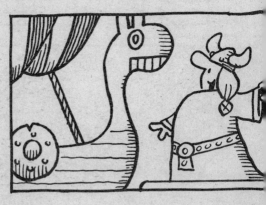

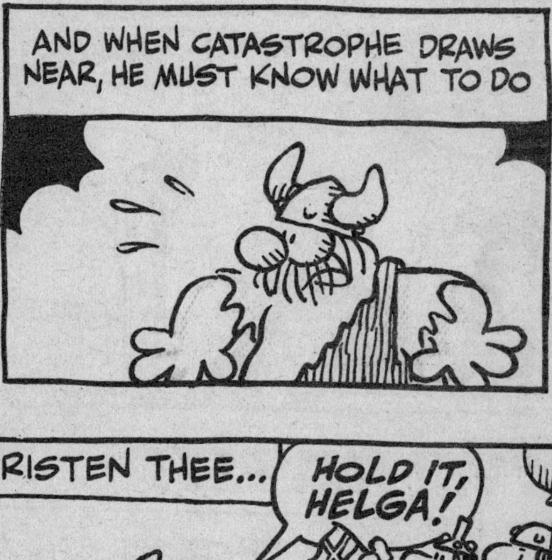
AND WHEN CATASTROPHE DRAWS NEAR, HE MUST KNOW WHAT TO DO

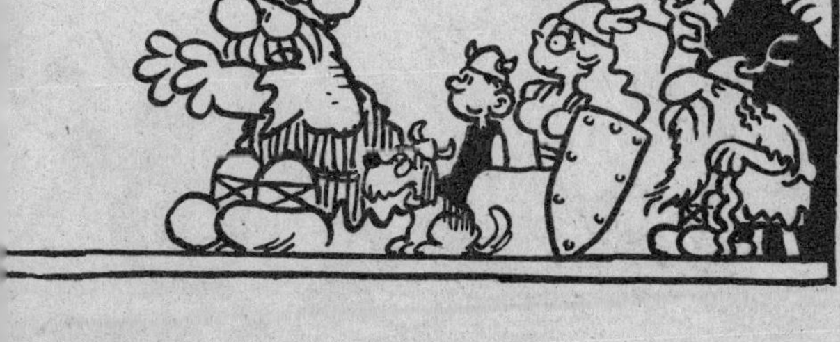
CHRISTEN THEE...
HOLD IT, HELGA!

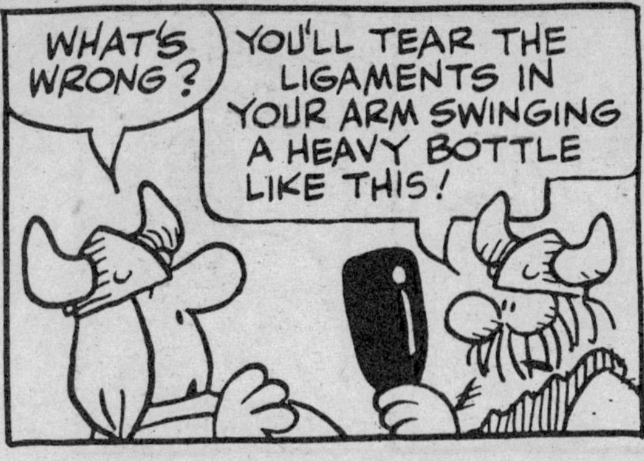
WHAT'S WRONG?
YOU'LL TEAR THE LIGAMENTS IN YOUR ARM SWINGING A HEAVY BOTTLE LIKE THIS!

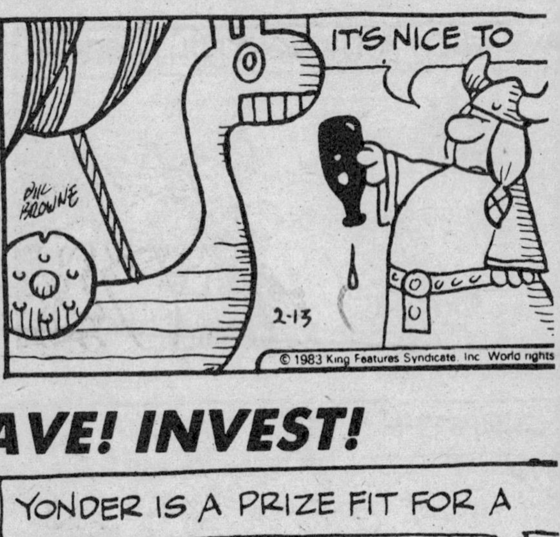
IT'S NICE TO
DIK BROWNE
2-13
© 1983 King Features Syndicate, Inc. World rights

SAVE! INVEST!

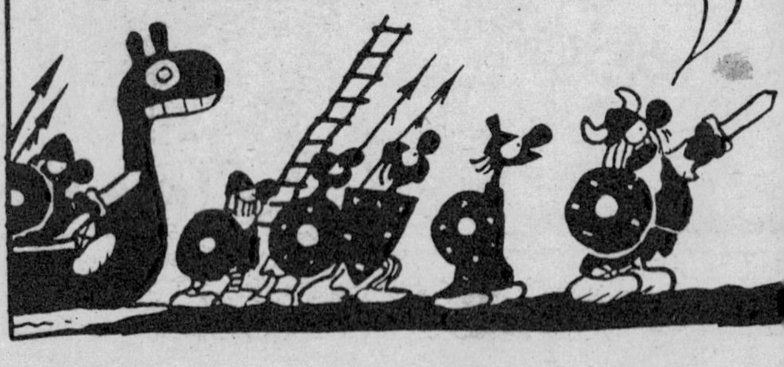
YONDER IS A PRIZE FIT FOR A

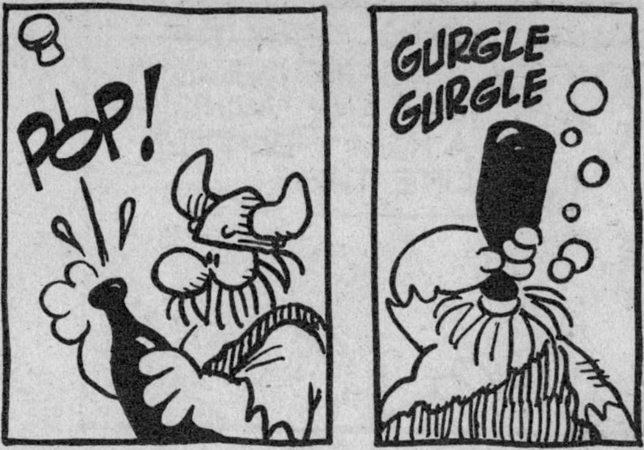
POP!
GURGLE GURGLE

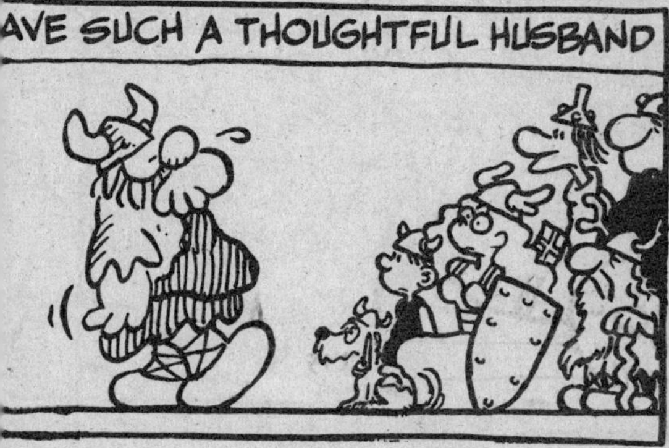
AVE SUCH A THOUGHTFUL HUSBAND

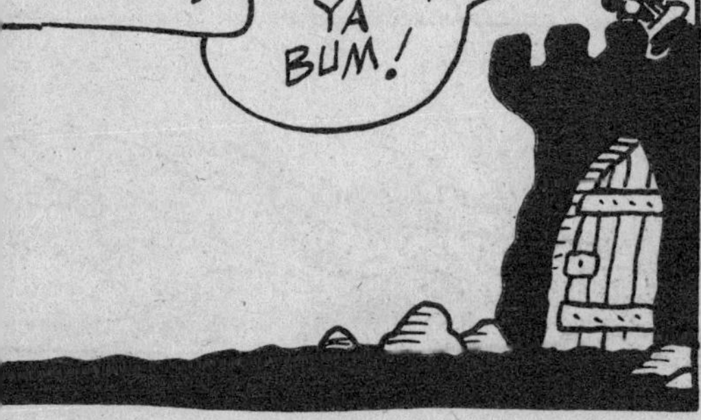
VIKING!
SCRAM, YA BUM!

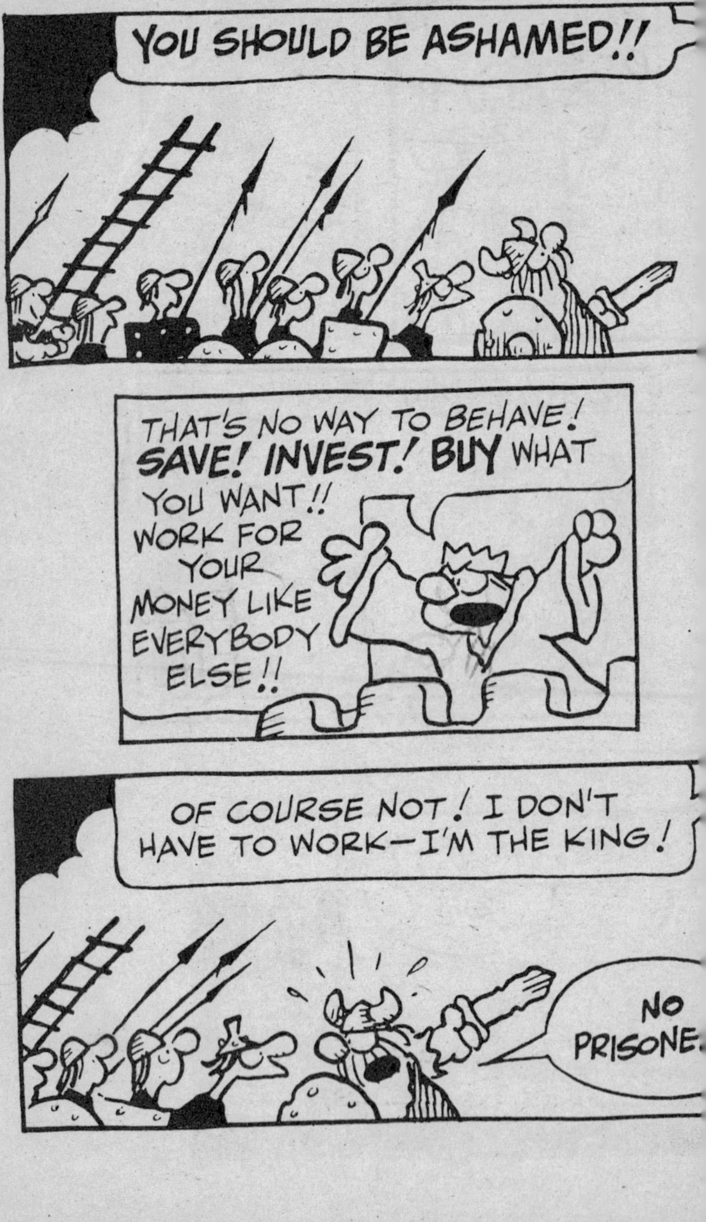
YOU SHOULD BE ASHAMED!!
THAT'S NO WAY TO BEHAVE! SAVE! INVEST! BUY WHAT YOU WANT!! WORK FOR YOUR MONEY LIKE EVERYBODY ELSE!!
OF COURSE NOT! I DON'T HAVE TO WORK—I'M THE KING!
NO PRISONE

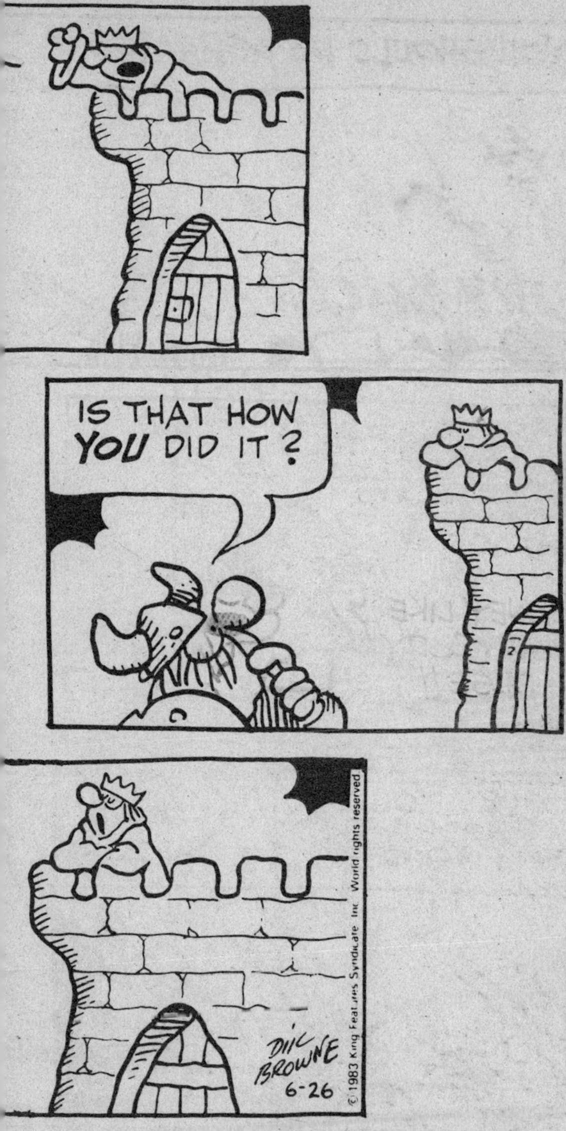
IS THAT HOW *YOU* DID IT?
DIK BROWNE 6-26
© 1983 King Features Syndicate, Inc. World rights reserved.

PICTURE SHOW

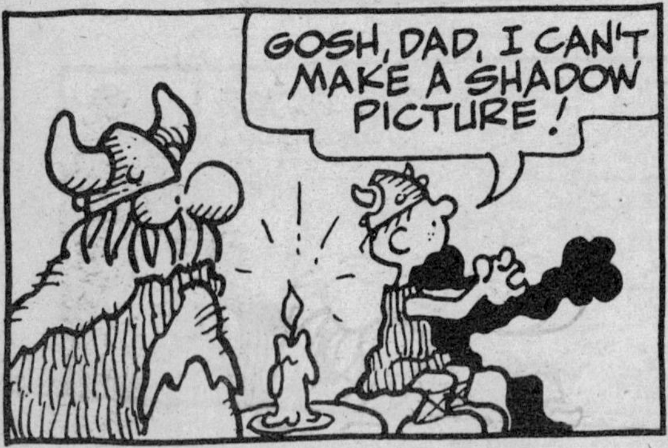
GOSH, DAD, I CAN'T MAKE A SHADOW PICTURE!

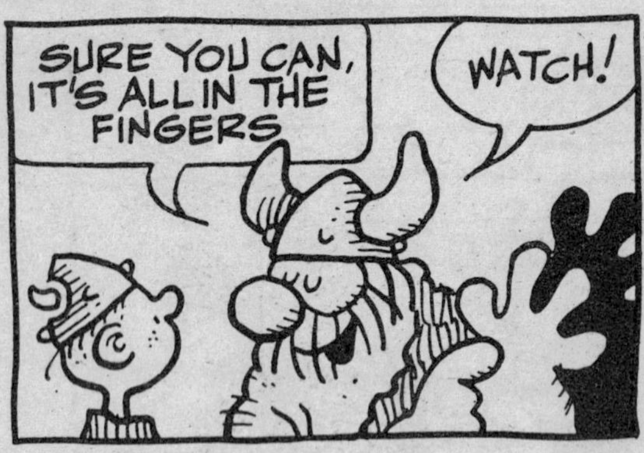
SURE YOU CAN, IT'S ALL IN THE FINGERS
WATCH!

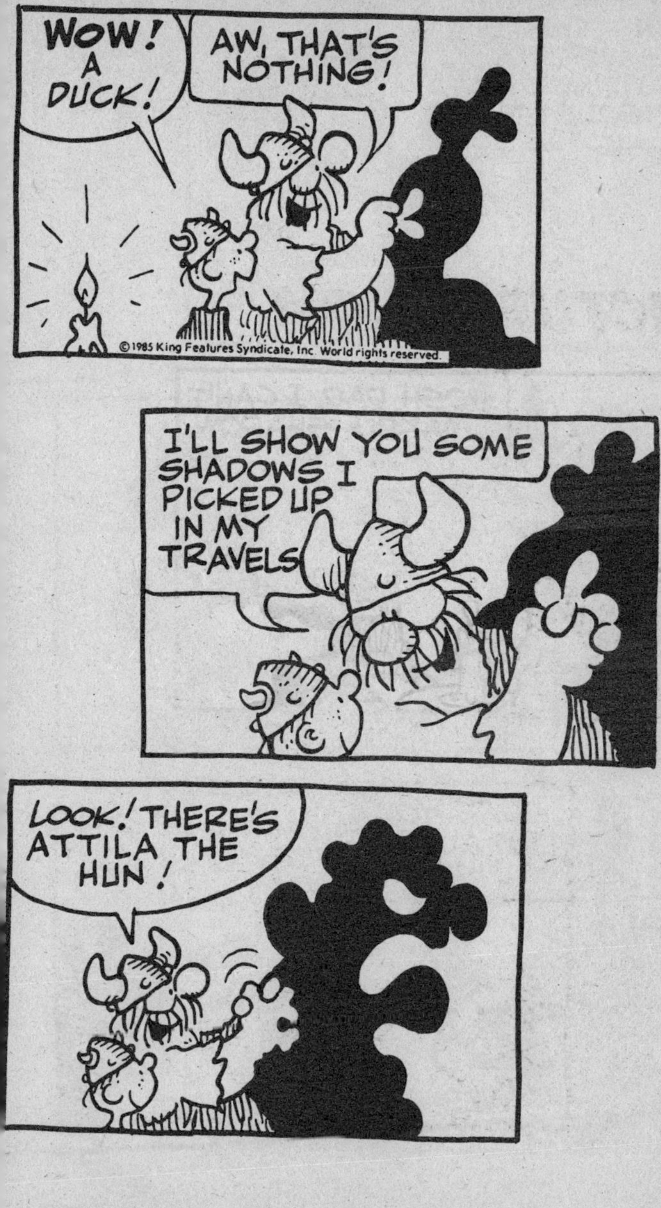
WOW! A DUCK!
AW, THAT'S NOTHING!
I'LL SHOW YOU SOME SHADOWS I PICKED UP IN MY TRAVELS
LOOK! THERE'S ATTILA THE HUN!

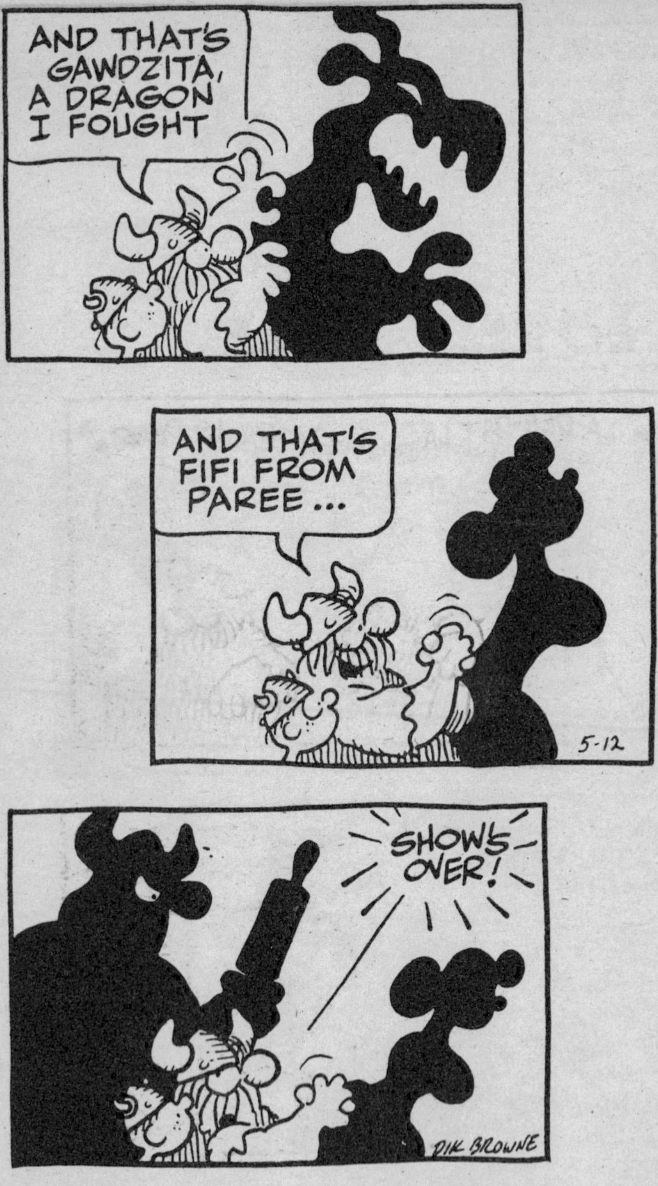
AND THAT'S GAWDZITA, A DRAGON I FOUGHT
AND THAT'S FIFI FROM PAREE ...
5-12
SHOW'S OVER!
DIK BROWNE

A LOVELY SMILE

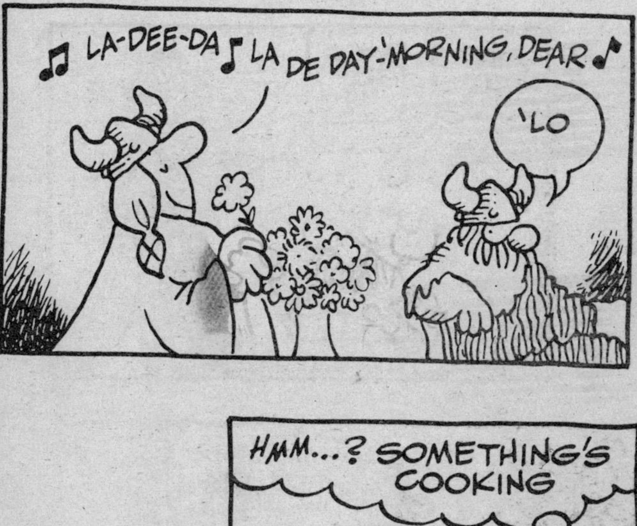
LA-DEE-DA LA DE DAY-MORNING, DEAR
'LO

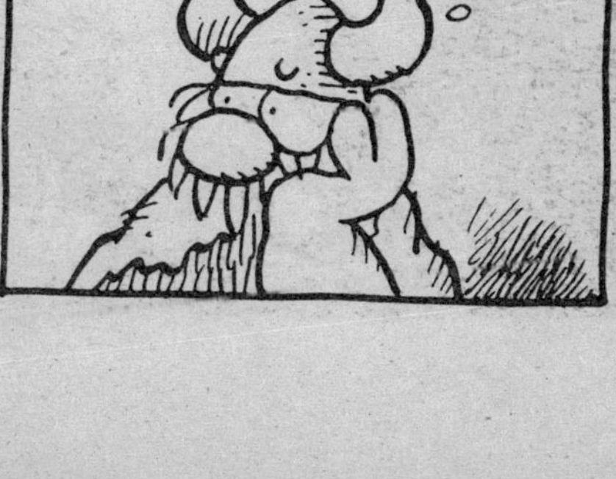
HMM...? SOMETHING'S COOKING

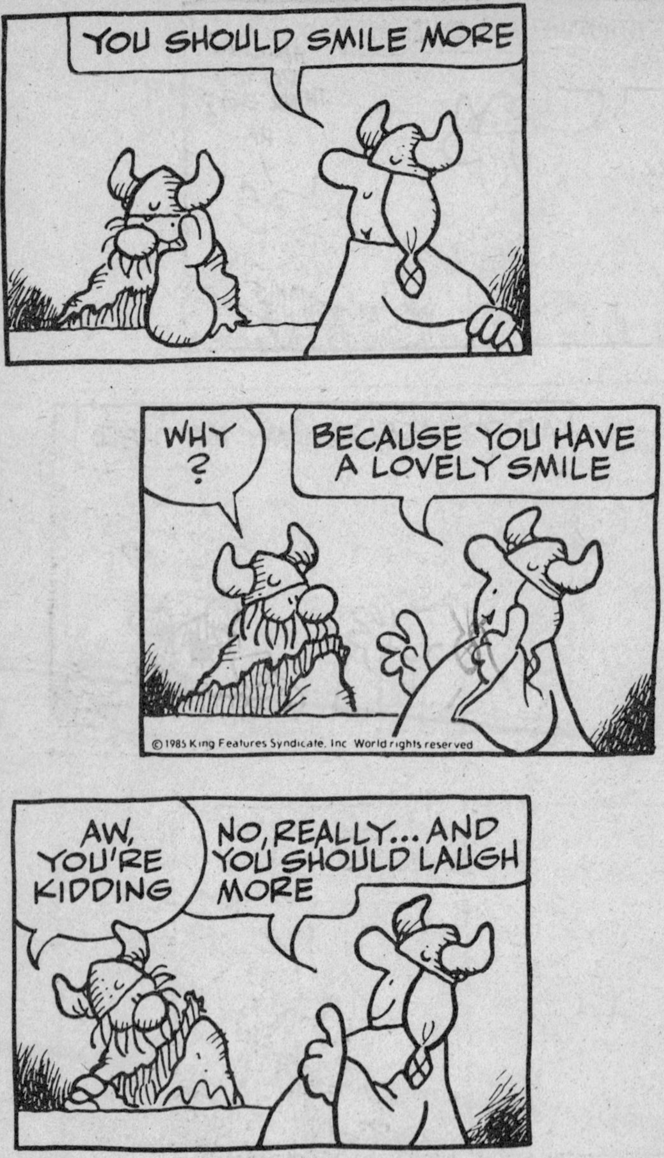
YOU SHOULD SMILE MORE
WHY ?
BECAUSE YOU HAVE A LOVELY SMILE
AW, YOU'RE KIDDING
NO, REALLY... AND YOU SHOULD LAUGH MORE

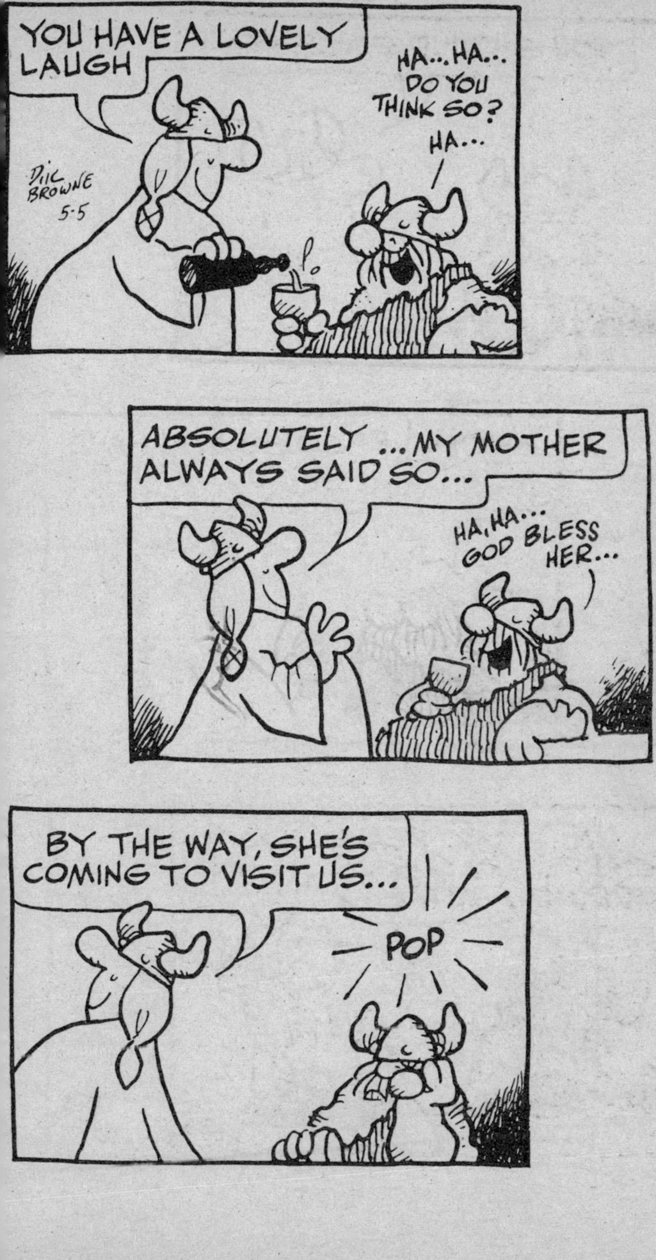
YOU HAVE A LOVELY LAUGH
HA... HA... DO YOU THINK SO? HA...
DIK BROWNE 5-5
ABSOLUTELY ...MY MOTHER ALWAYS SAID SO...
HA, HA... GOD BLESS HER...
BY THE WAY, SHE'S COMING TO VISIT US...
POP

SPRINGTIME

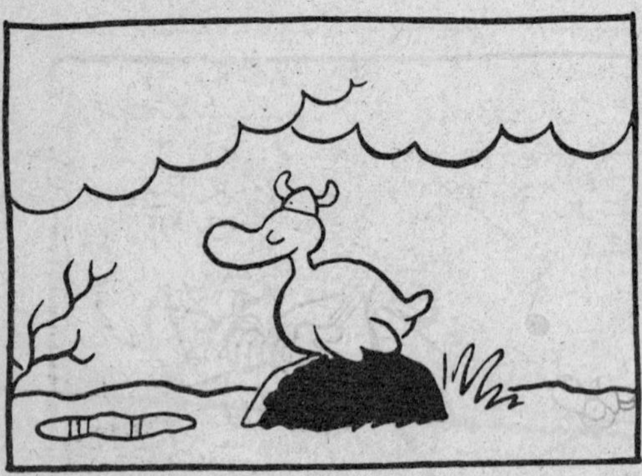

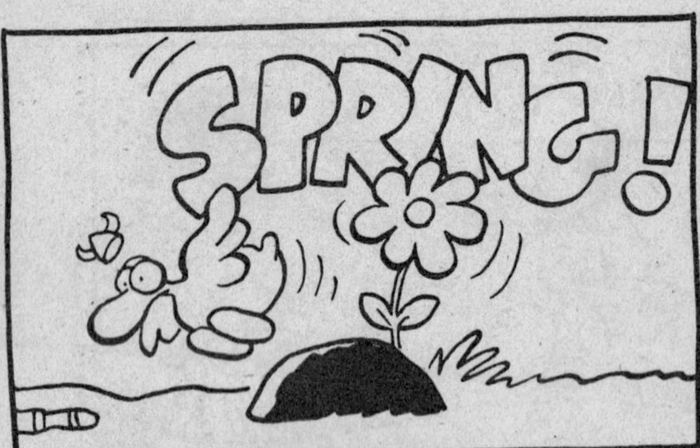
SPRING!

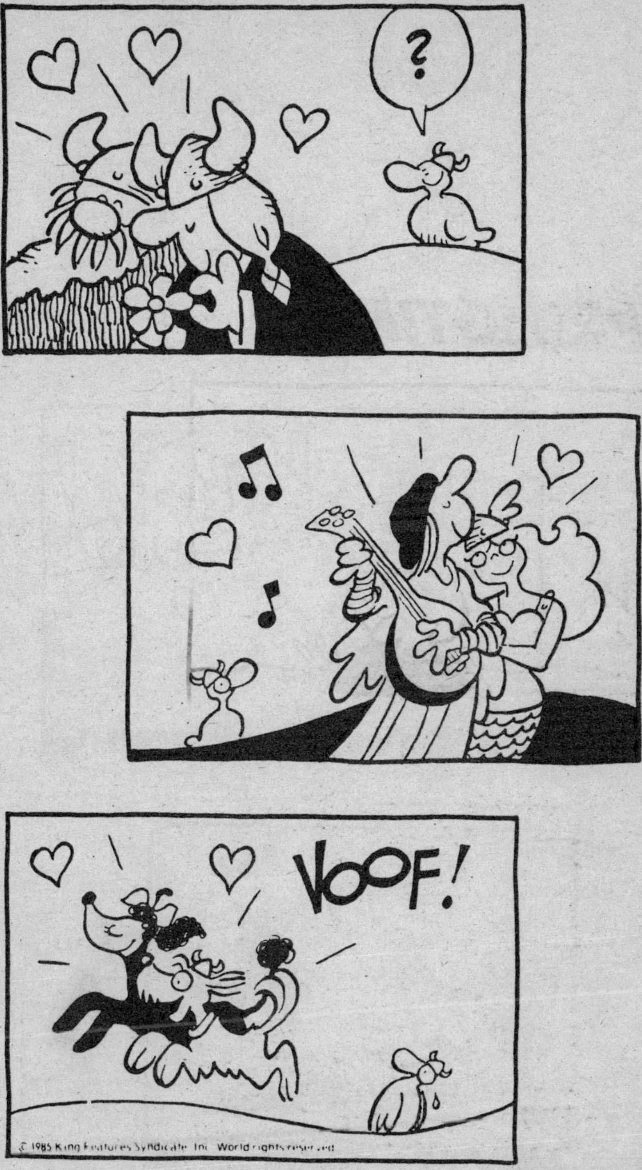
?
VOOF!
© 1985 King Features Syndicate, Inc. World rights reserved.

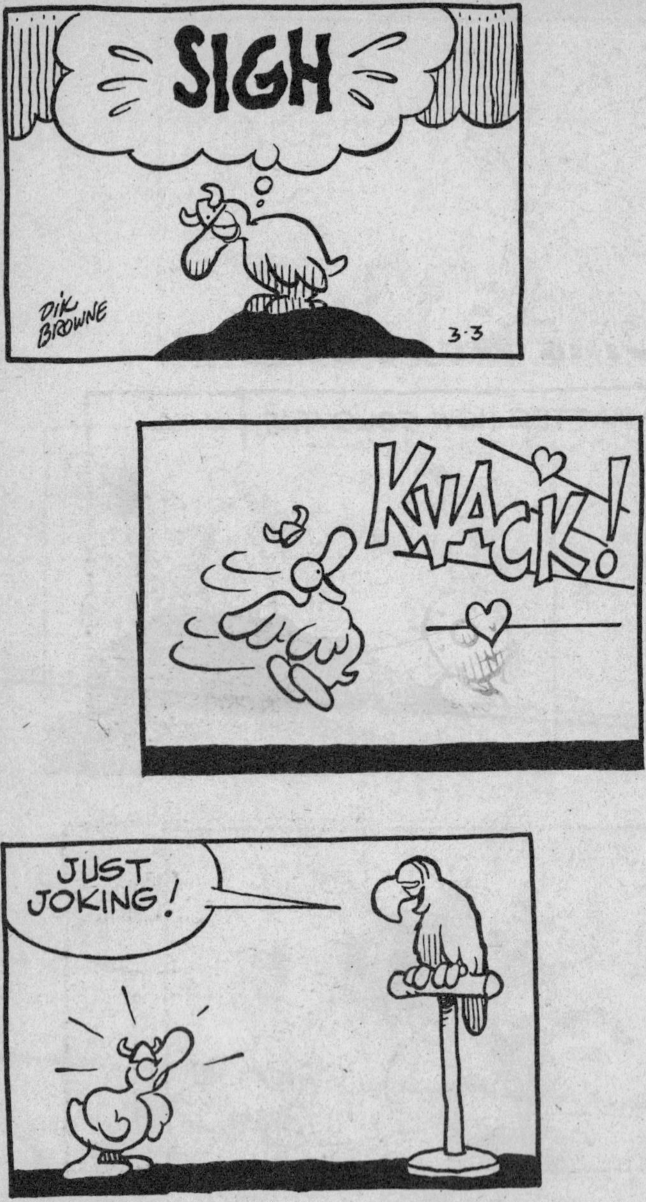
SIGH
DIK BROWNE
3-3
KWACK!
JUST JOKING!

SOME WELCOME

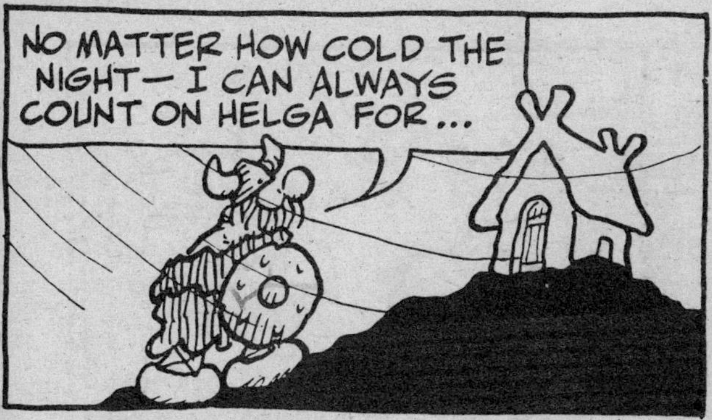
NO MATTER HOW COLD THE NIGHT— I CAN ALWAYS COUNT ON HELGA FOR...

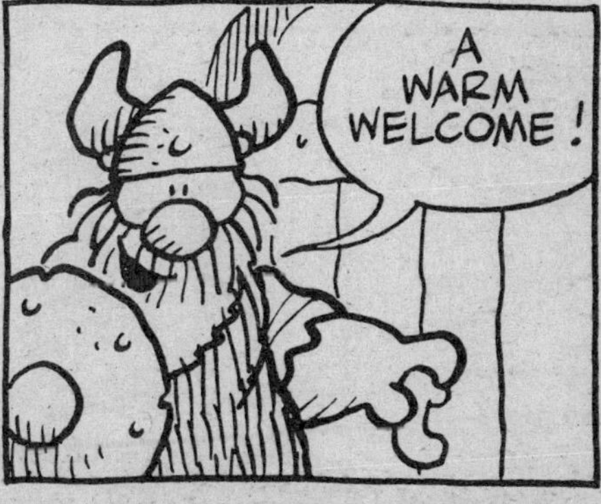
A WARM WELCOME!

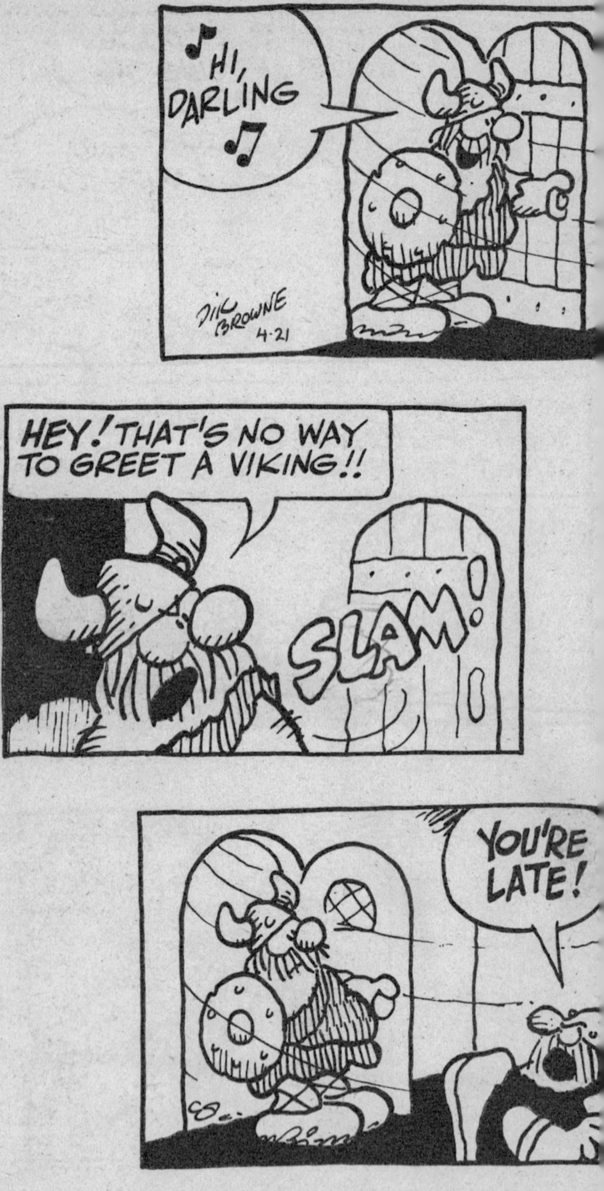
HI, DARLING
DIK BROWNE 4·21
HEY! THAT'S NO WAY TO GREET A VIKING!!
SLAM!
YOU'RE LATE!

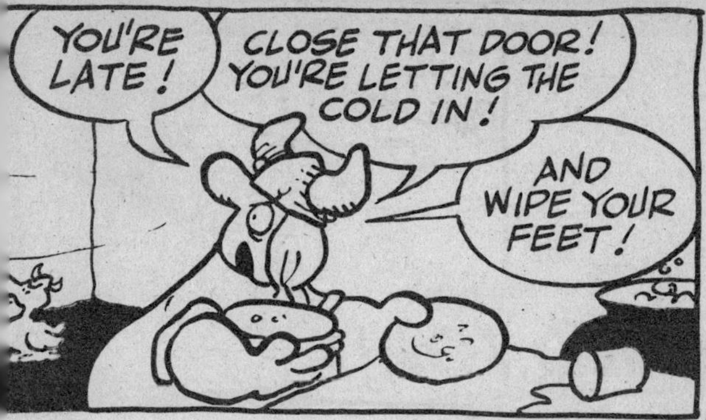
YOU'RE LATE!
CLOSE THAT DOOR! YOU'RE LETTING THE COLD IN!
AND WIPE YOUR FEET!

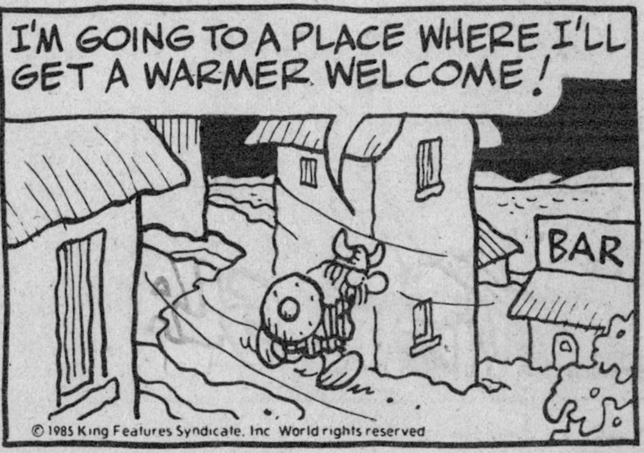
I'M GOING TO A PLACE WHERE I'LL GET A WARMER WELCOME!
BAR

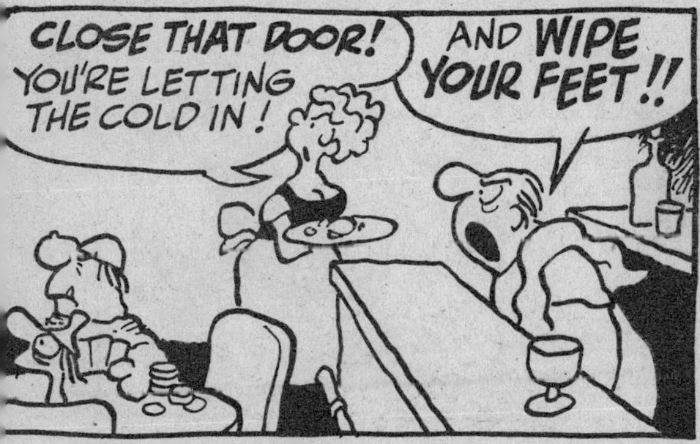
CLOSE THAT DOOR! YOU'RE LETTING THE COLD IN!
AND WIPE YOUR FEET!!

HORNED TOAD

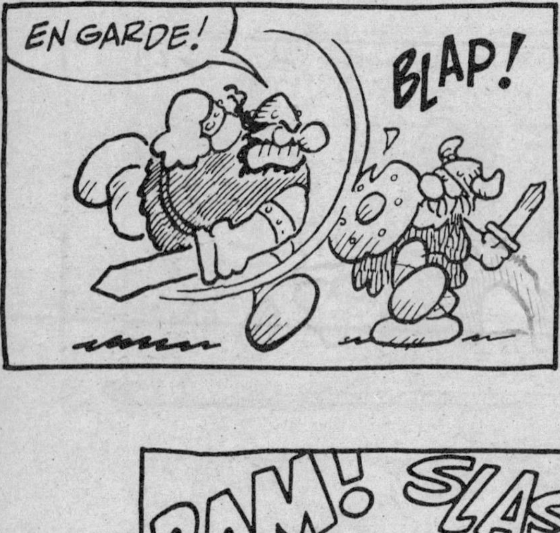
EN GARDE!
BLAP!

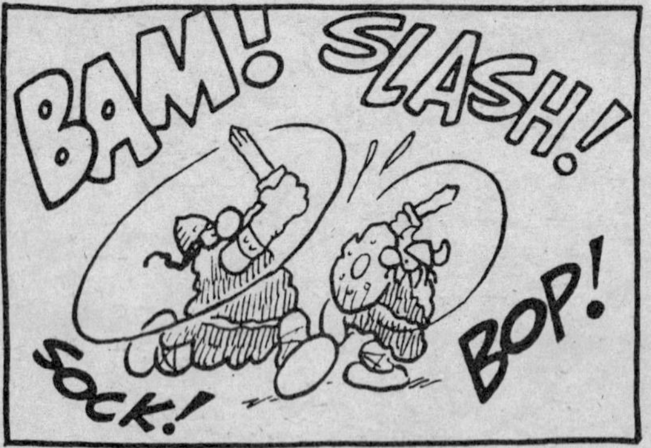
BAM!
SLASH!
SOCK!
BOP!

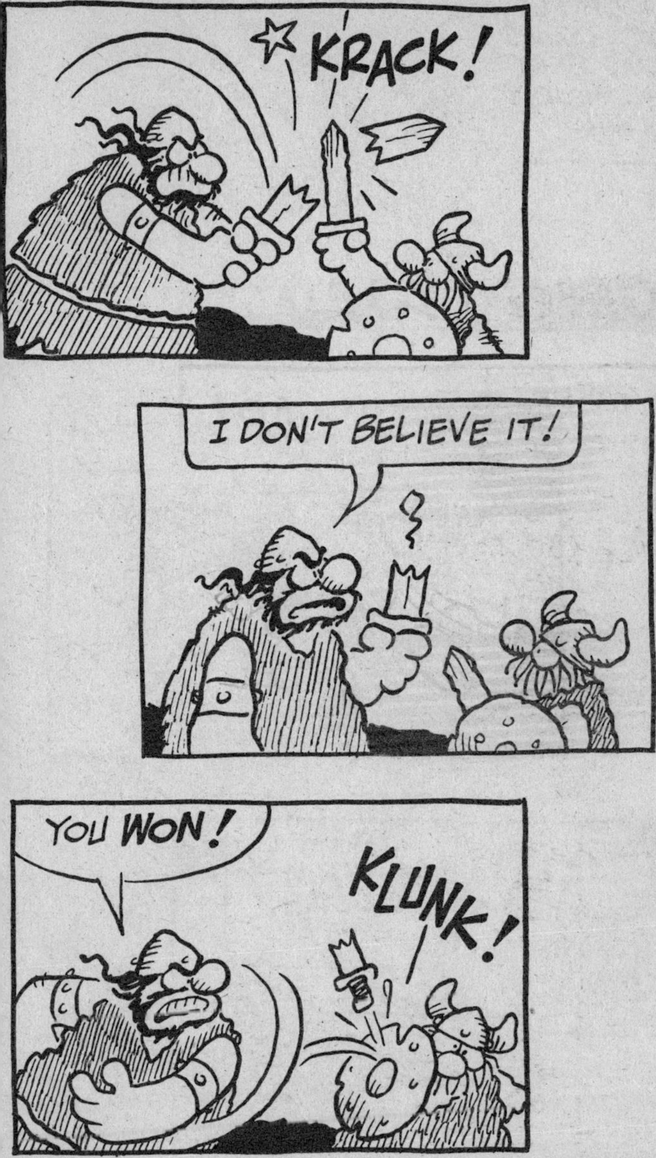
KRACK!
I DON'T BELIEVE IT!
YOU WON!
KLUNK!

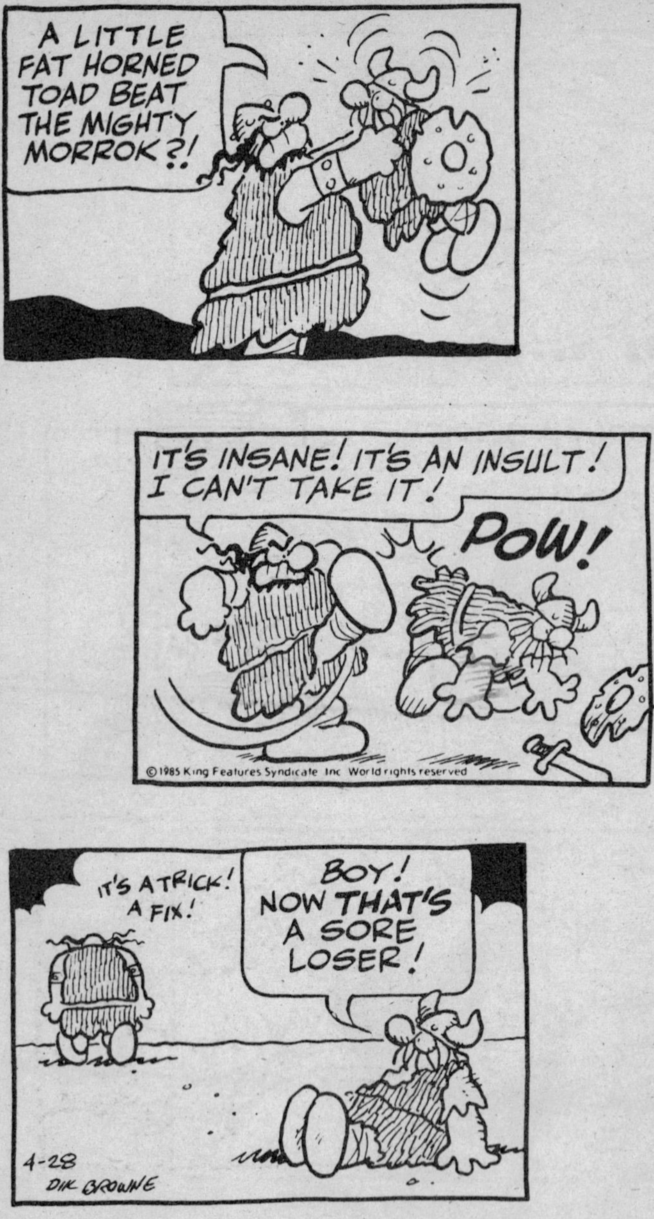
A LITTLE FAT HORNED TOAD BEAT THE MIGHTY MORROK ?!
IT'S INSANE! IT'S AN INSULT! I CAN'T TAKE IT!
POW!
© 1985 King Features Syndicate Inc World rights reserved
IT'S A TRICK! A FIX!
BOY! NOW THAT'S A SORE LOSER!
4-28
DIK BROWNE

SPRING

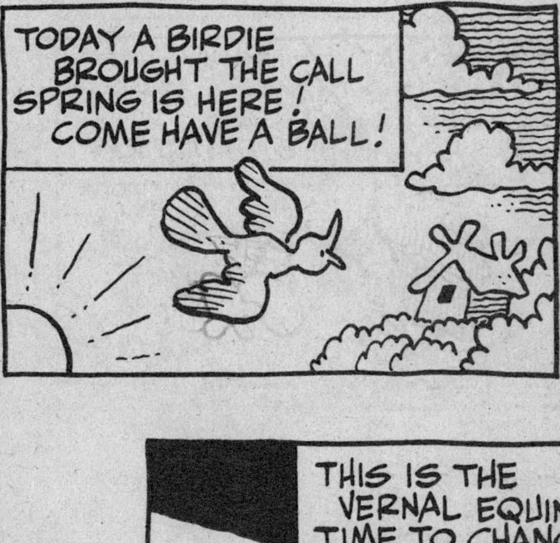
TODAY A BIRDIE
BROUGHT THE CALL
SPRING IS HERE!
COME HAVE A BALL!

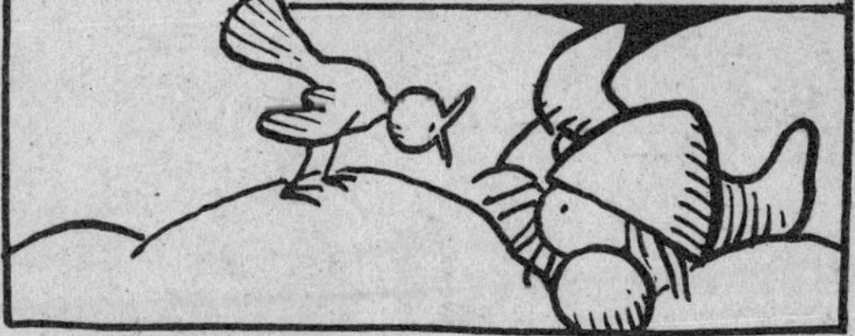
THIS IS THE
VERNAL EQUINOX
TIME TO CHANGE
YOUR DIRTY SOCKS

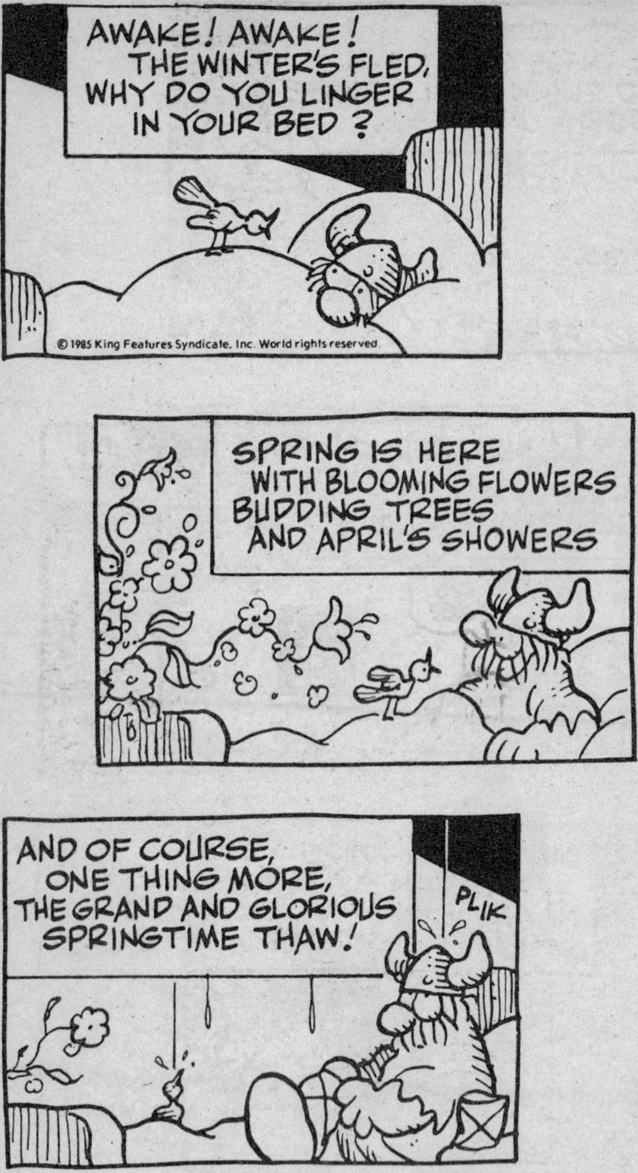
AWAKE! AWAKE! THE WINTER'S FLED, WHY DO YOU LINGER IN YOUR BED?
© 1985 King Features Syndicate, Inc. World rights reserved.
SPRING IS HERE WITH BLOOMING FLOWERS BUDDING TREES AND APRIL'S SHOWERS
AND OF COURSE, ONE THING MORE, THE GRAND AND GLORIOUS SPRINGTIME THAW!
PLIK

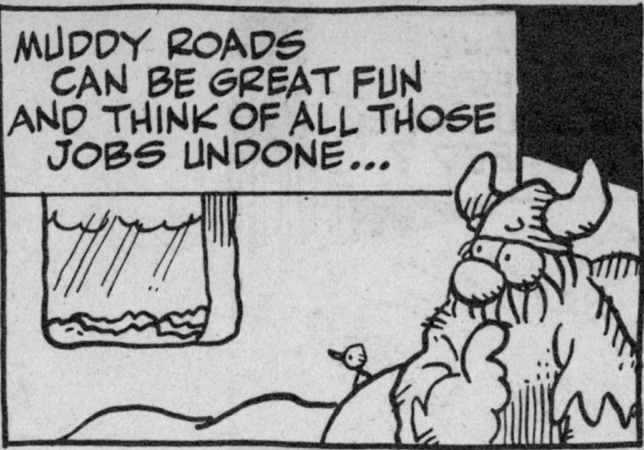
MUDDY ROADS
CAN BE GREAT FUN
AND THINK OF ALL THOSE
JOBS UNDONE...

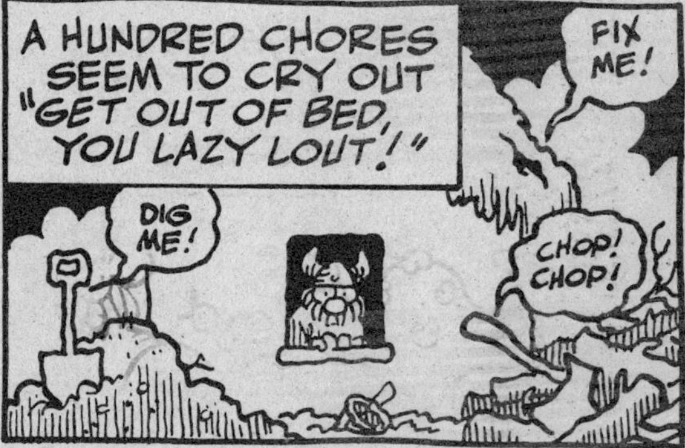
A HUNDRED CHORES
SEEM TO CRY OUT
"GET OUT OF BED,
YOU LAZY LOUT!"
FIX ME!
DIG ME!
CHOP! CHOP!

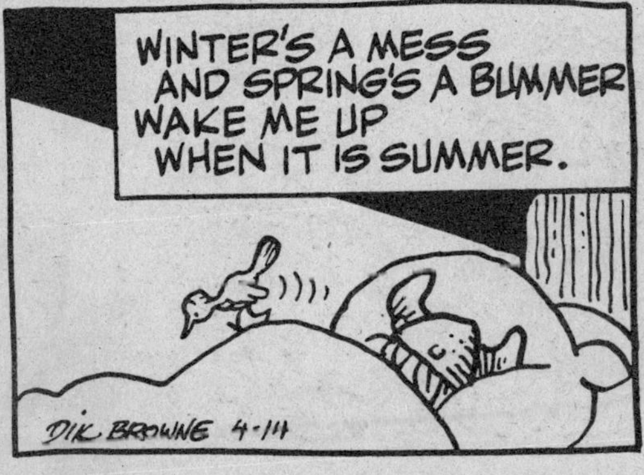
WINTER'S A MESS
AND SPRING'S A BUMMER
WAKE ME UP
WHEN IT IS SUMMER.
DIK BROWNE 4-11

BAD LUCK

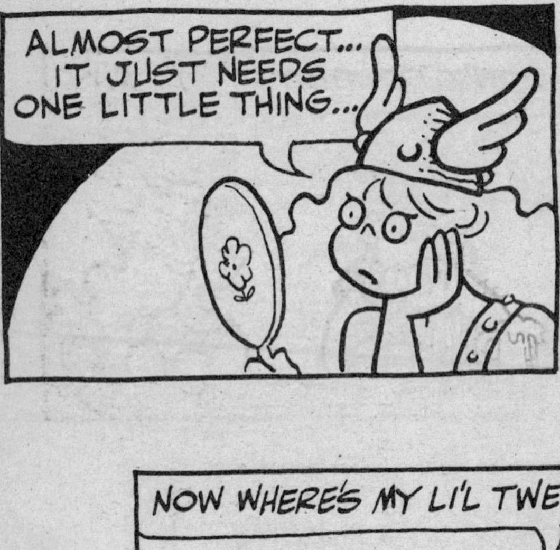
ALMOST PERFECT... IT JUST NEEDS ONE LITTLE THING...

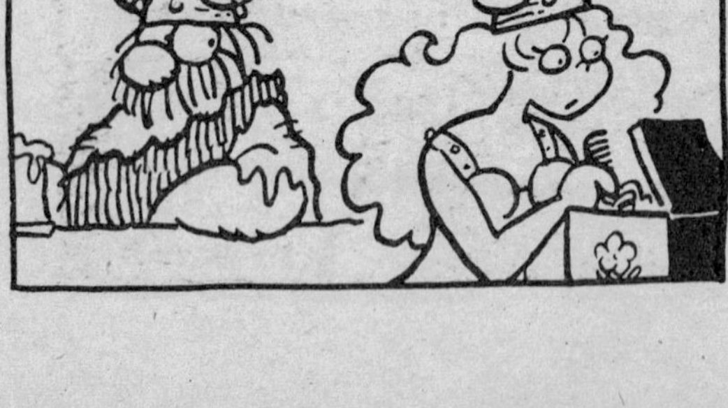
NOW WHERE'S MY LI'L TWEEZER?

WHAT ARE YOU DOING, HONI ?
JUST PLUCKING A HAIR...
DON'T DO THAT!
WHY ?
© 1985 King Features Syndicate, Inc World rights reserved
IF YOU PLUCK A HAIR, TEN WILL COME TO ITS FUNERAL
DIK BROWNE

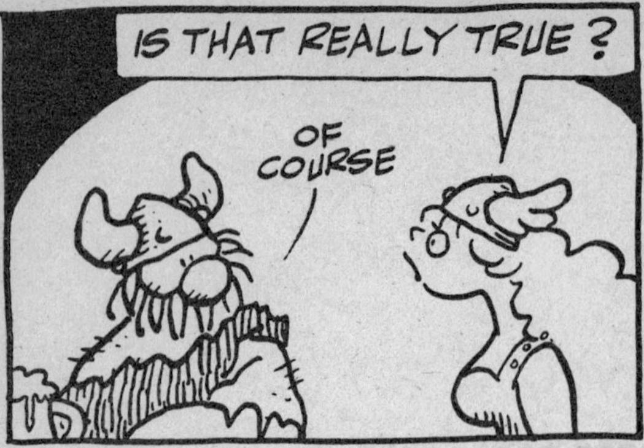
IS THAT REALLY TRUE ?
OF COURSE

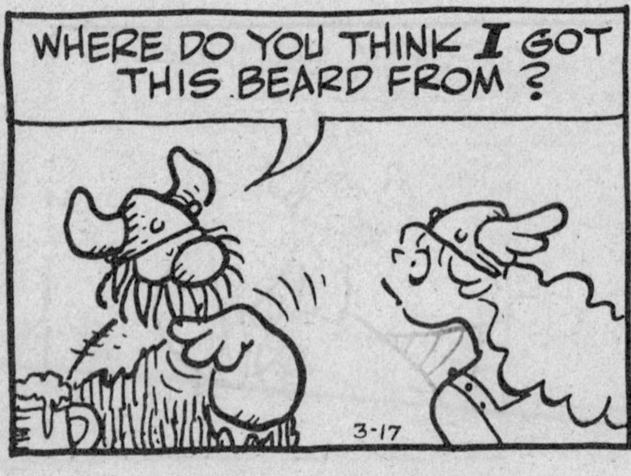
WHERE DO YOU THINK I GOT THIS BEARD FROM ?
3-17

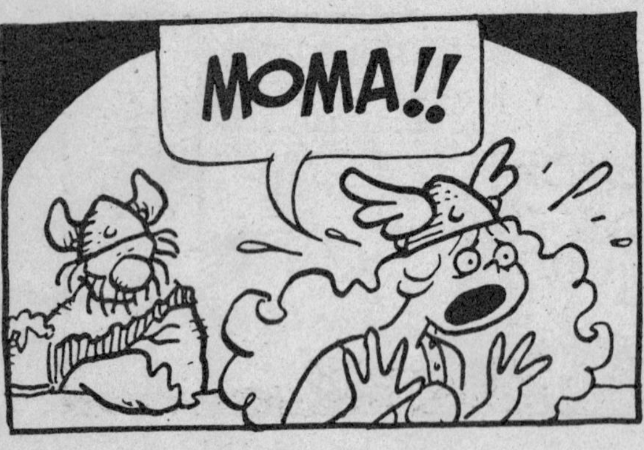
MOMA!!

OVERWORKED

COOK! COOK! COOK! IT NEVER STOPS!
I KNOW... I'M HUNGRY, TOO...
KVACK? KVACK?!

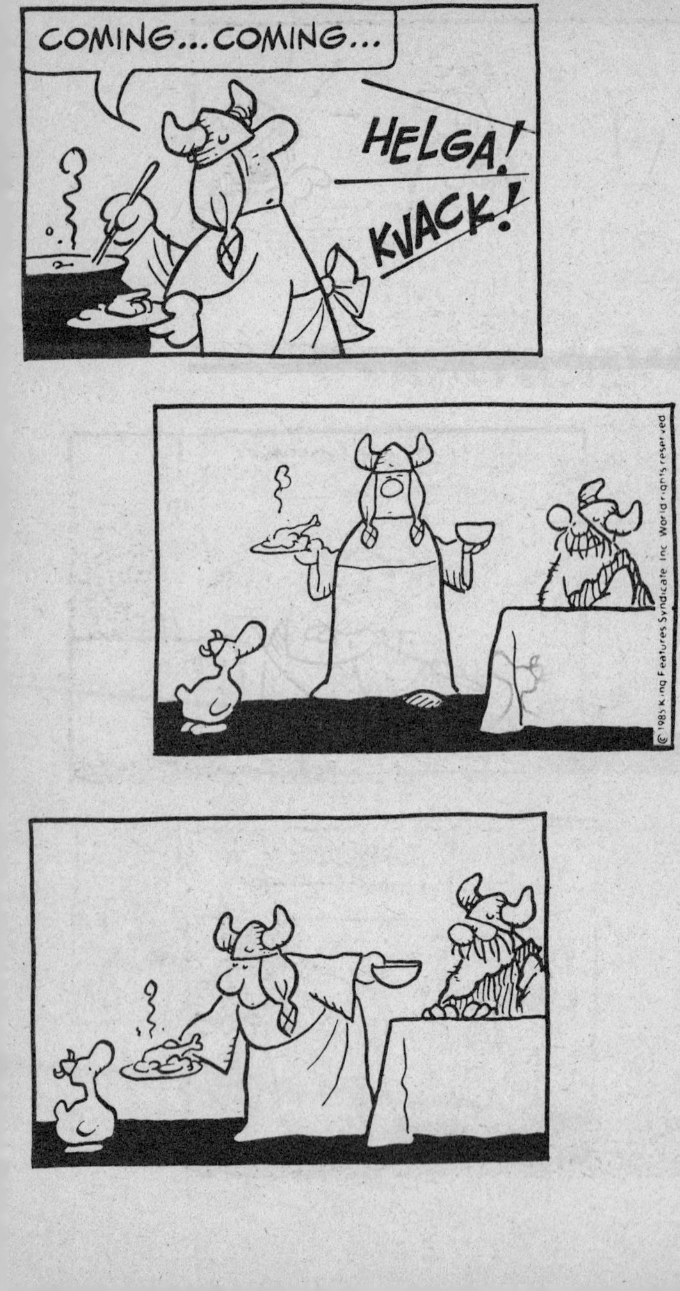
COMING...COMING...
HELGA!
KVACK!
© 1985 King Features Syndicate Inc World rights reserved

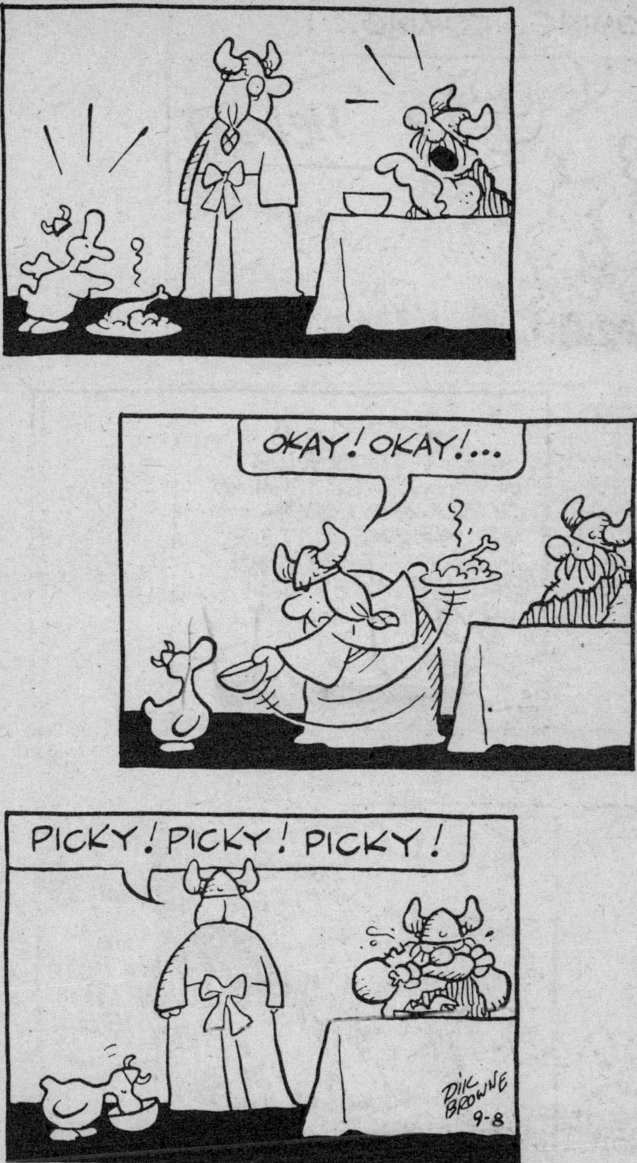
OKAY! OKAY!...
PICKY! PICKY! PICKY!
DIK BROWNE
9-8

WHAT A LIVING

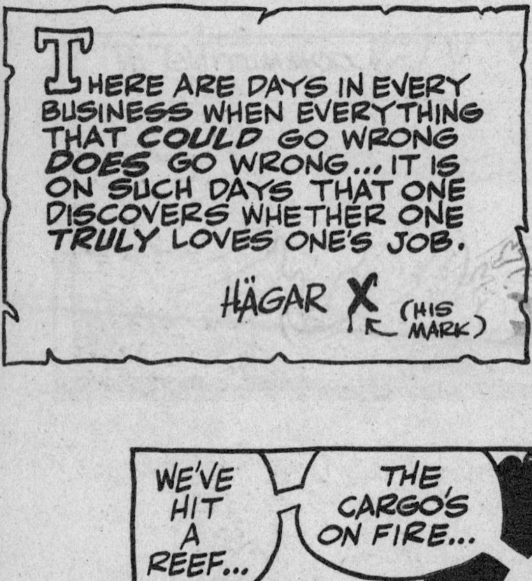
THERE ARE DAYS IN EVERY BUSINESS WHEN EVERYTHING THAT COULD GO WRONG DOES GO WRONG... IT IS ON SUCH DAYS THAT ONE DISCOVERS WHETHER ONE TRULY LOVES ONE'S JOB.
HÄGAR X
(HIS MARK)

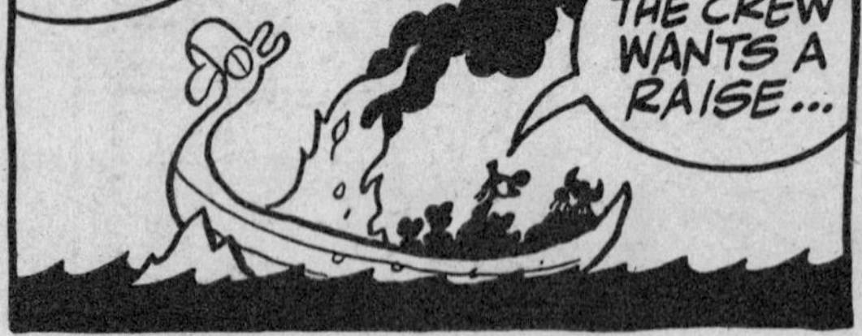
WE'VE HIT A REEF...
THE CARGO'S ON FIRE...
AND THE CREW WANTS A RAISE...

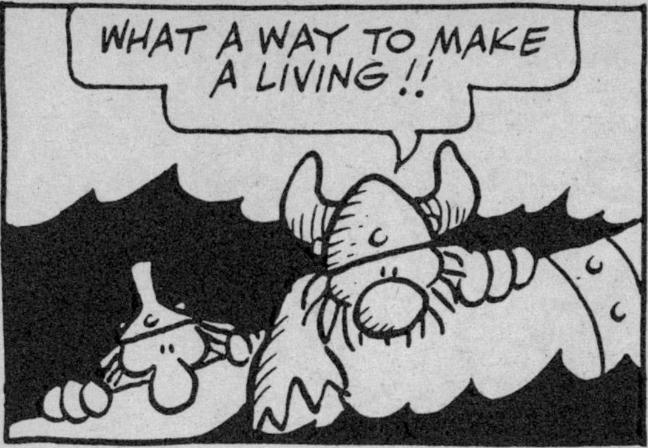
WHAT A WAY TO MAKE A LIVING !!

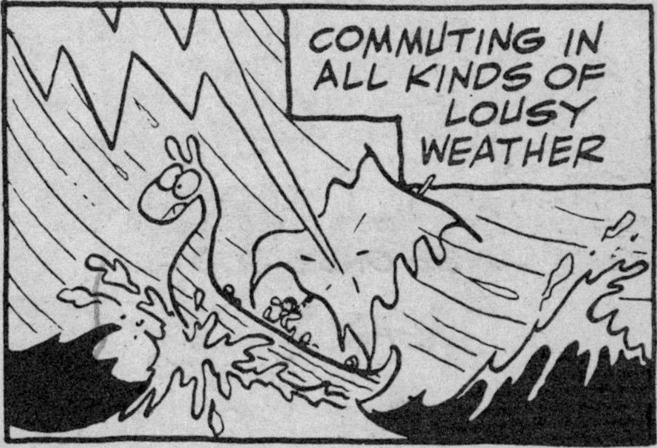
COMMUTING IN ALL KINDS OF LOUSY WEATHER

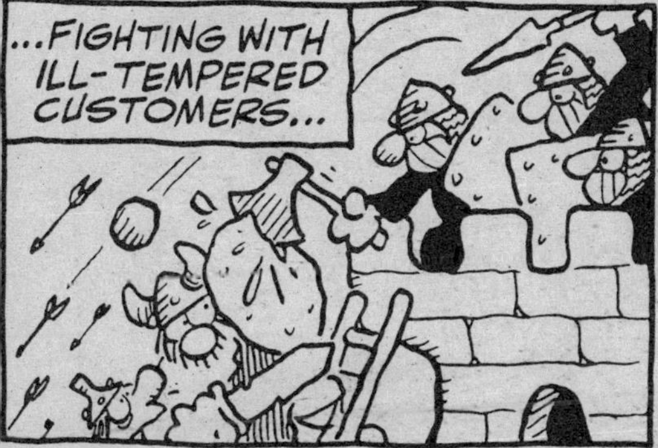
...FIGHTING WITH ILL-TEMPERED CUSTOMERS...

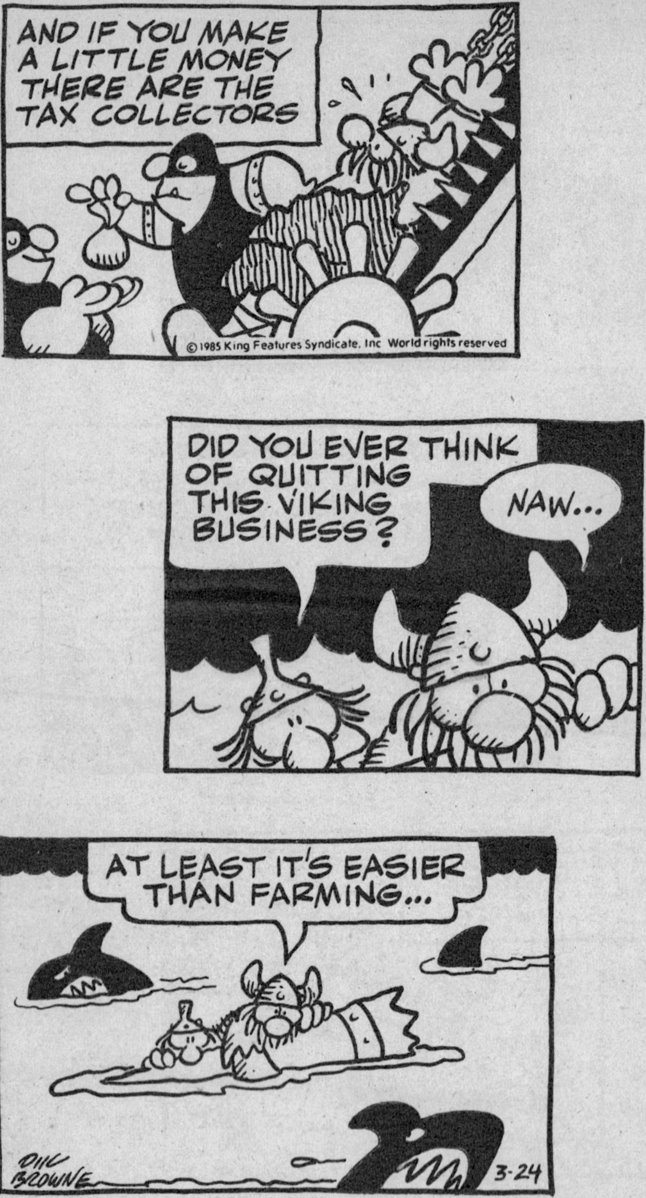
AND IF YOU MAKE A LITTLE MONEY THERE ARE THE TAX COLLECTORS
© 1985 King Features Syndicate, Inc World rights reserved
DID YOU EVER THINK OF QUITTING THIS VIKING BUSINESS?
NAW...
AT LEAST IT'S EASIER THAN FARMING...
DIK BROWNE
3-24

A MAN'S WORLD

I CAN'T GET ANYBODY TO GO PLUNDERING ANYMORE

THOR THE TERRIBLE IS BABY-SITTING ...MEAN MAX IS SHOPPING WITH HIS MISSUS, AND ERIC'S WIFE WON'T LET HIM GO...

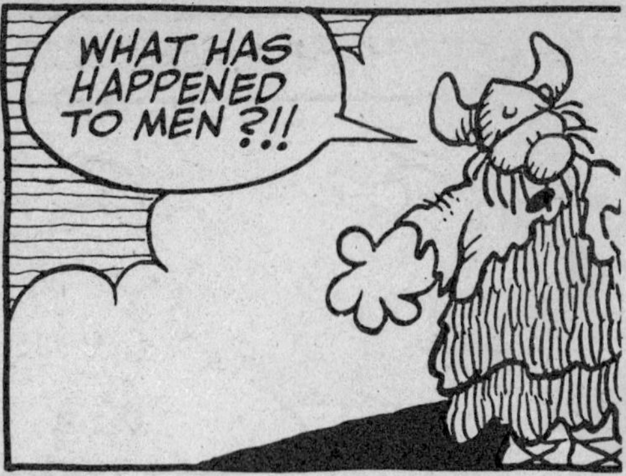
WHAT HAS HAPPENED TO MEN ?!!

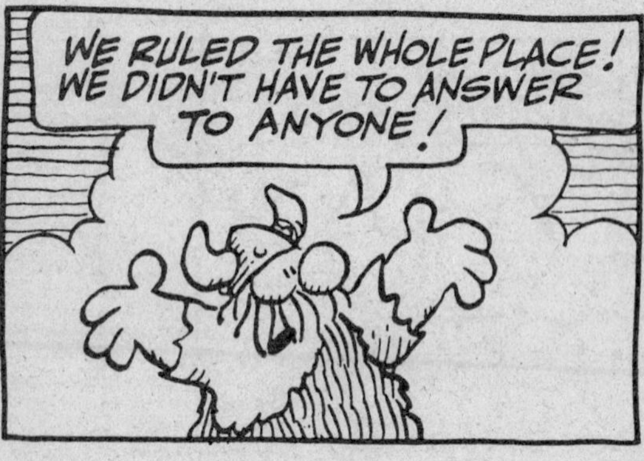
WE RULED THE WHOLE PLACE! WE DIDN'T HAVE TO ANSWER TO ANYONE!

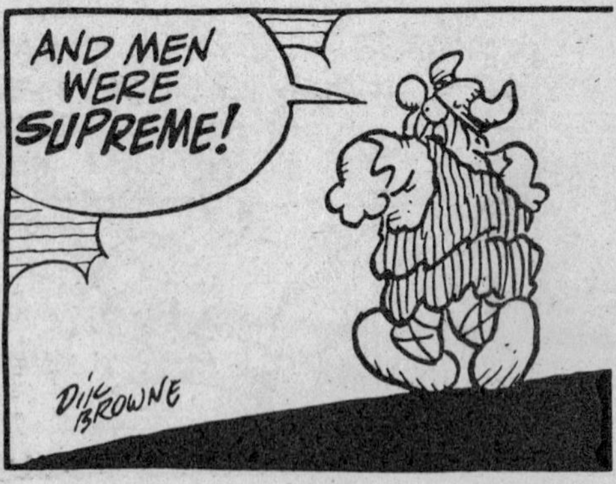
AND MEN WERE SUPREME!
DIK BROWNE

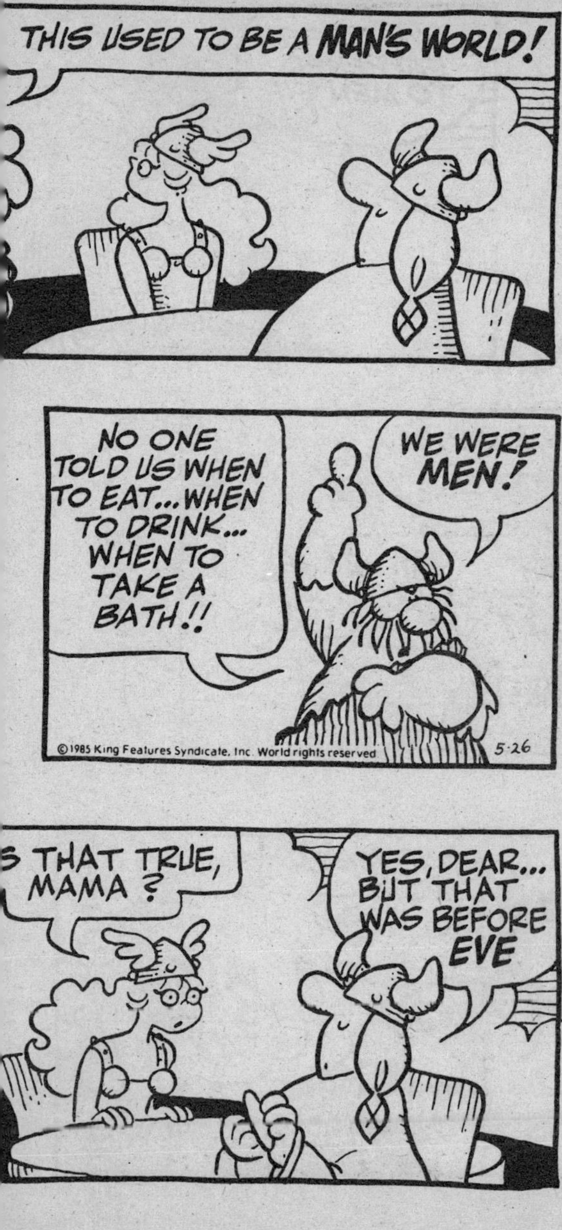
THIS USED TO BE A MAN'S WORLD!
NO ONE TOLD US WHEN TO EAT...WHEN TO DRINK... WHEN TO TAKE A BATH!!
WE WERE MEN!
©1985 King Features Syndicate, Inc. World rights reserved
5·26
S THAT TRUE, MAMA ?
YES, DEAR... BUT THAT WAS BEFORE EVE

BIG IDEAS

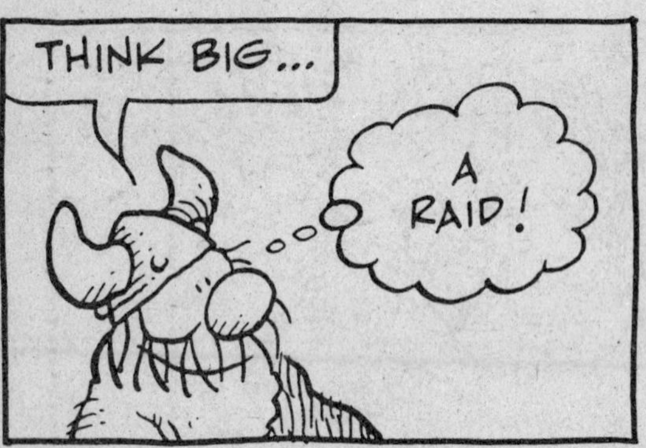
THINK BIG...
A RAID!

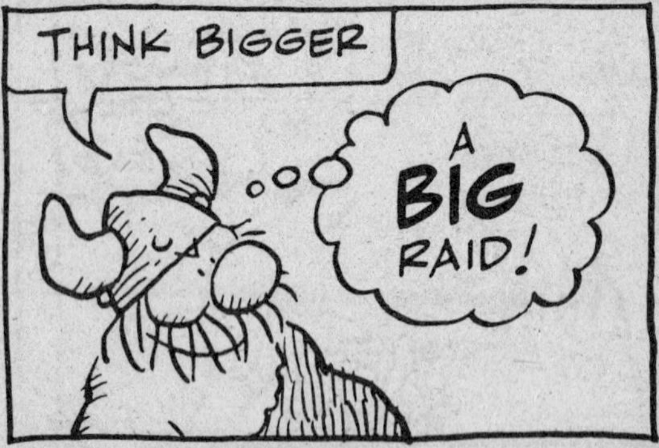
THINK BIGGER
A BIG RAID!

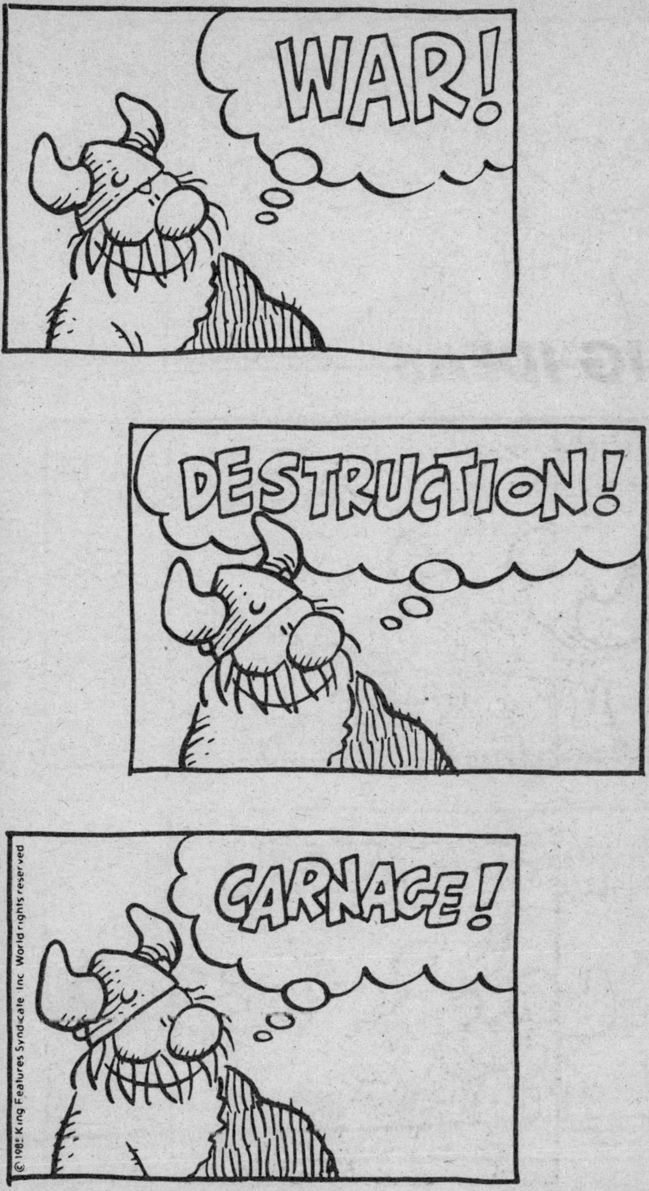
WAR!
DESTRUCTION!
CARNAGE!
© 1985 King Features Syndicate Inc World rights reserved

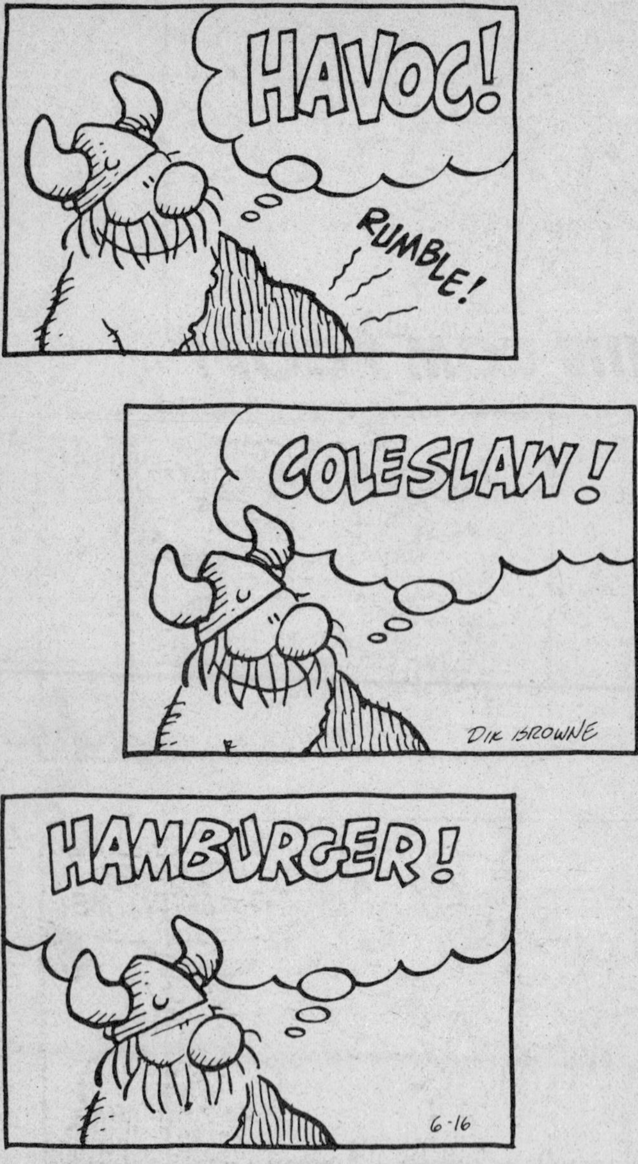
HAVOC!
RUMBLE!
COLESLAW!
DIK BROWNE
HAMBURGER!
6-16

NIN COM POOP!

I'M HUNGRY! LET'S STOP AND EAT LUNCH
LUNCH ??
DON'T TELL ME! PLEASE DON'T TELL ME!

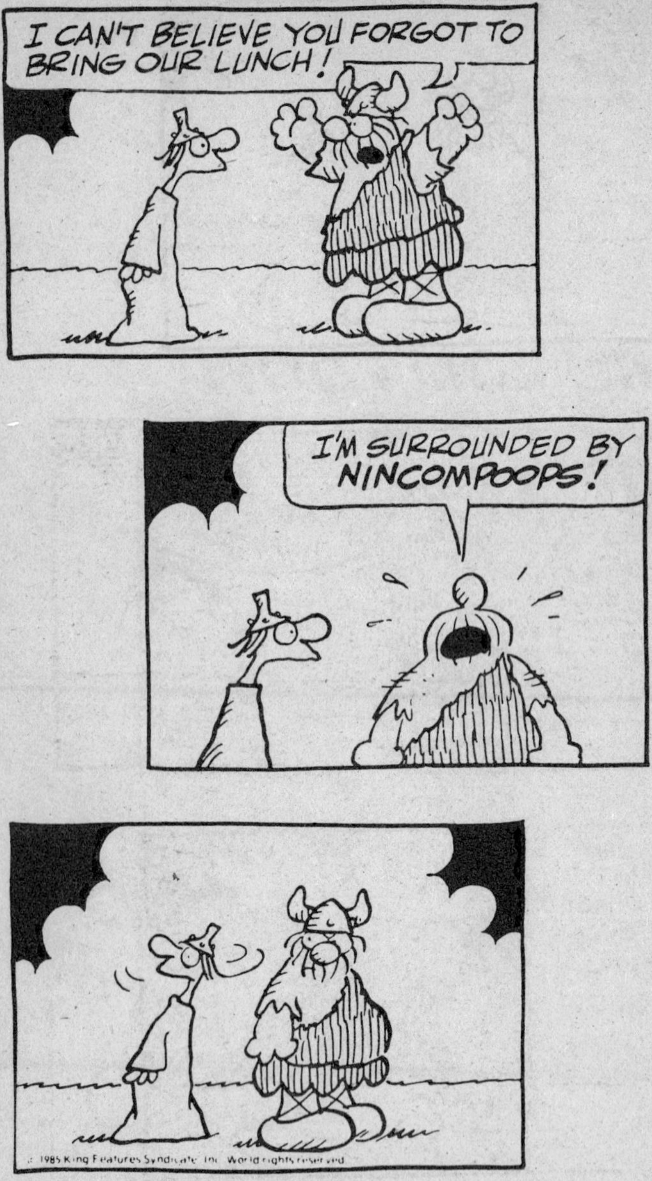
I CAN'T BELIEVE YOU FORGOT TO BRING OUR LUNCH!
I'M SURROUNDED BY NINCOMPOOPS!

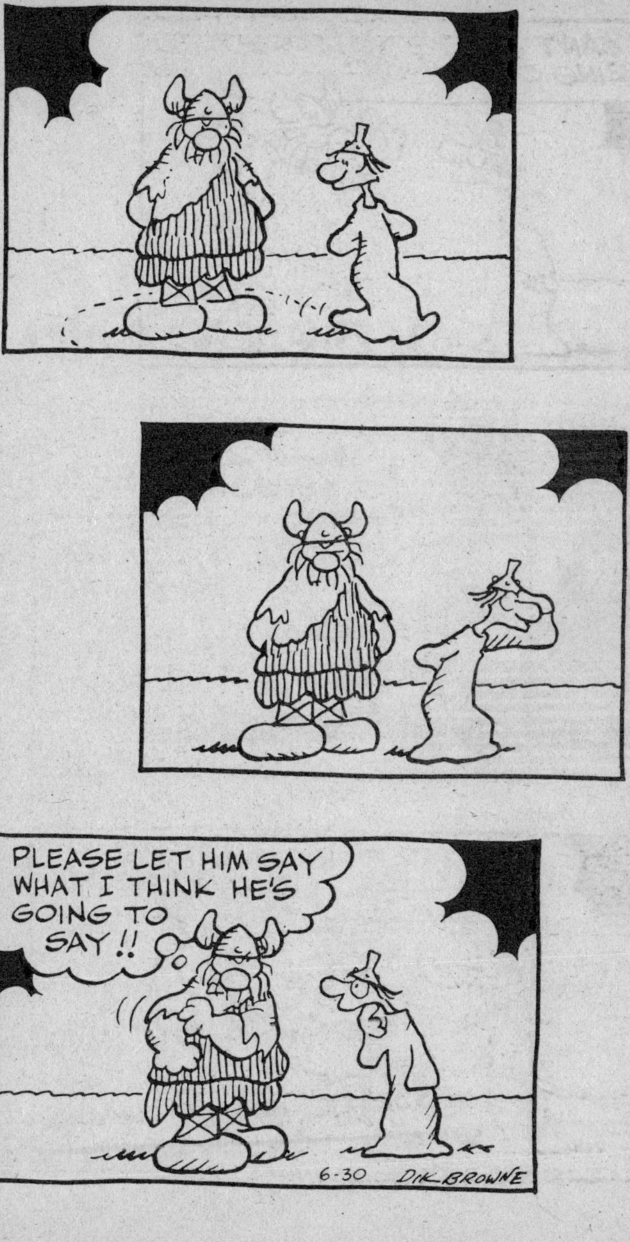
PLEASE LET HIM SAY WHAT I THINK HE'S GOING TO SAY !!
6-30 DIK BROWNE

MERRY OLD ENGLAND

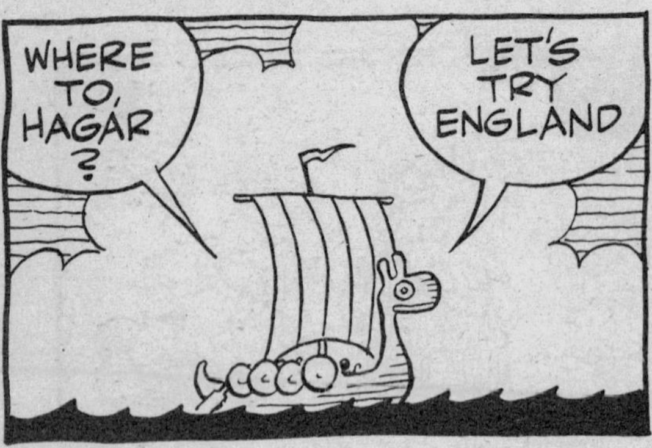
WHERE TO, HAGAR ?
LET'S TRY ENGLAND

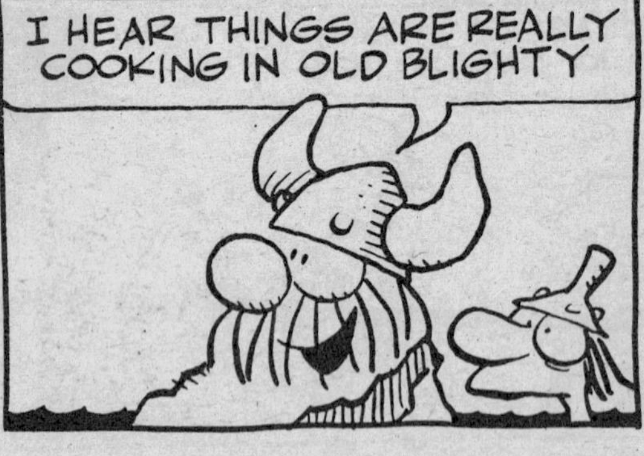
I HEAR THINGS ARE REALLY COOKING IN OLD BLIGHTY

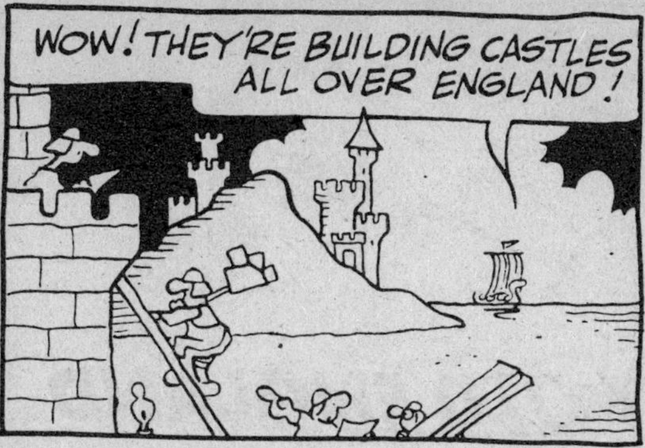
WOW! THEY'RE BUILDING CASTLES ALL OVER ENGLAND!

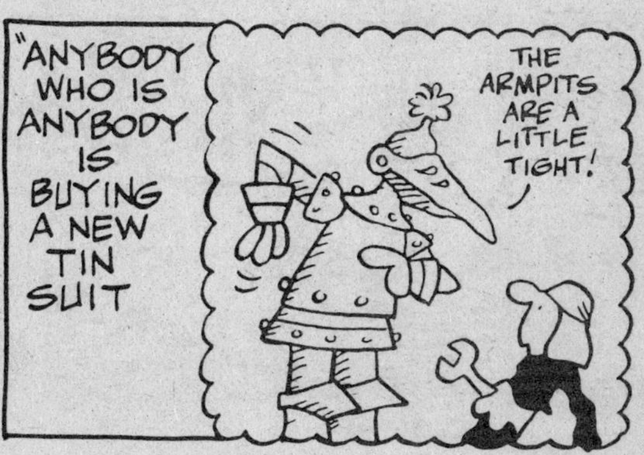
"ANYBODY WHO IS ANYBODY IS BUYING A NEW TIN SUIT
THE ARMPITS ARE A LITTLE TIGHT!

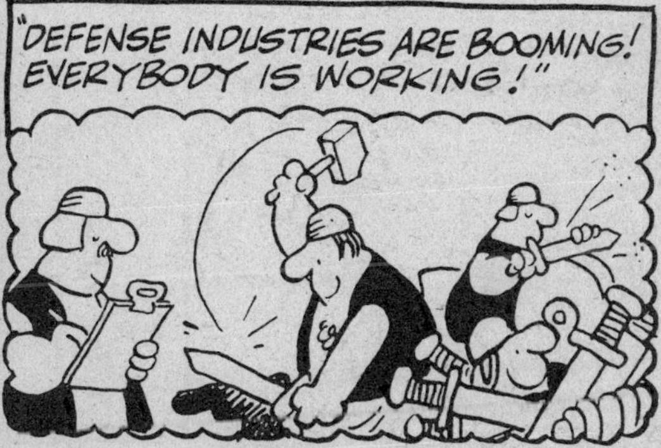
"DEFENSE INDUSTRIES ARE BOOMING! EVERYBODY IS WORKING!"

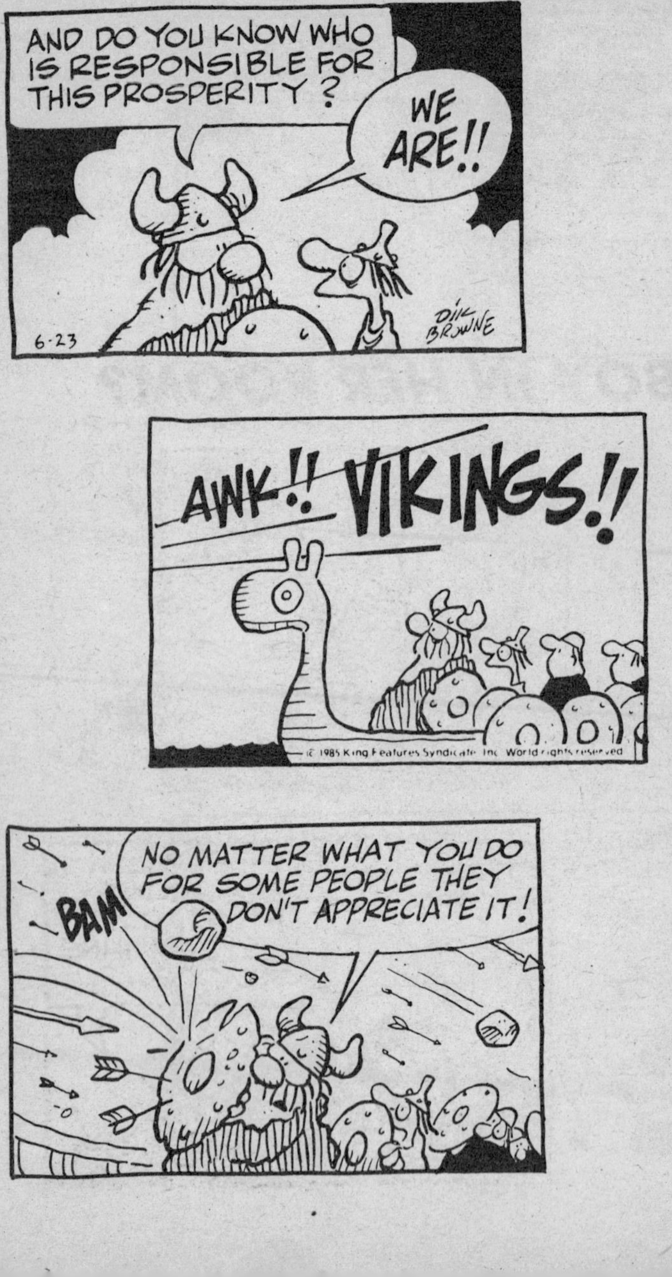

AND DO YOU KNOW WHO IS RESPONSIBLE FOR THIS PROSPERITY ?
WE ARE!!
6-23
DIK BROWNE
AWK!! VIKINGS!!
© 1985 King Features Syndicate, Inc. World rights reserved
BAM
NO MATTER WHAT YOU DO FOR SOME PEOPLE THEY DON'T APPRECIATE IT!

BOY IN HER ROOM?

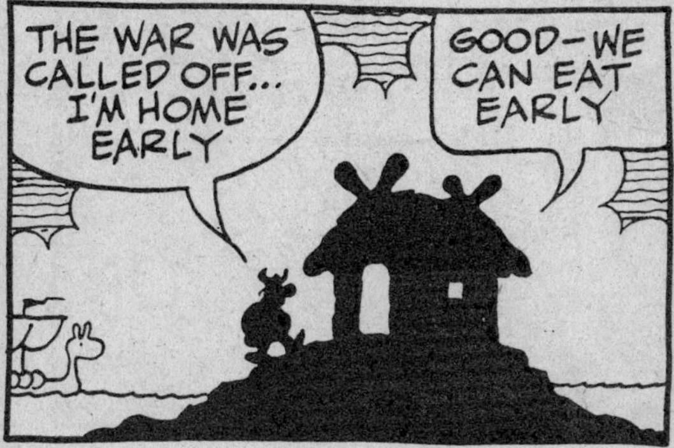
THE WAR WAS CALLED OFF... I'M HOME EARLY
GOOD—WE CAN EAT EARLY

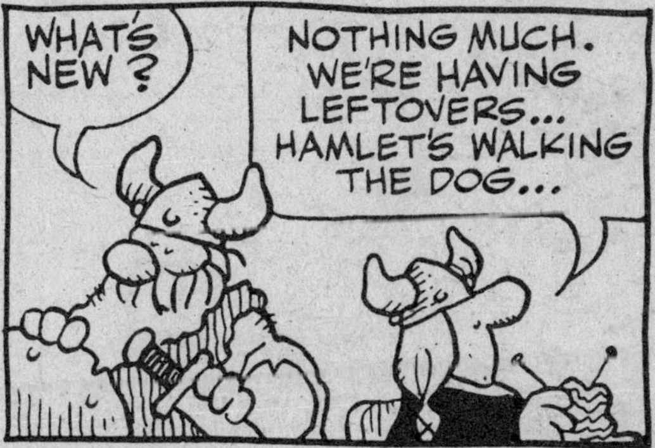
WHAT'S NEW ?
NOTHING MUCH. WE'RE HAVING LEFTOVERS... HAMLET'S WALKING THE DOG...

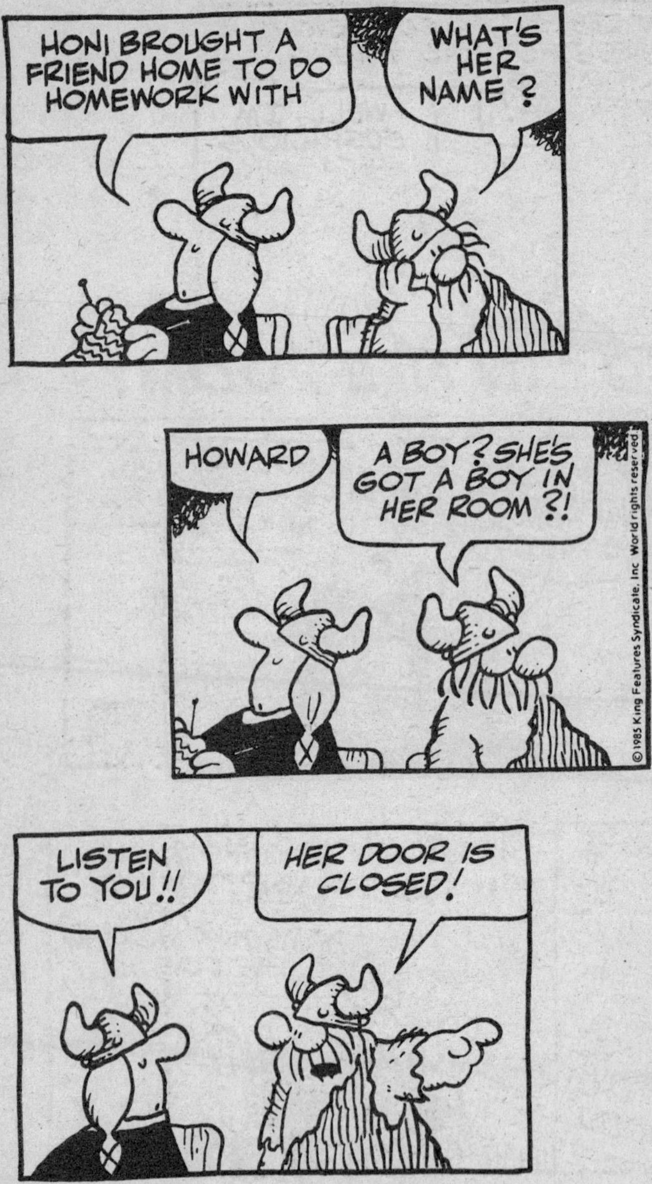
HONI BROUGHT A FRIEND HOME TO DO HOMEWORK WITH
WHAT'S HER NAME?
HOWARD
A BOY? SHE'S GOT A BOY IN HER ROOM?!
© 1985 King Features Syndicate, Inc. World rights reserved.
LISTEN TO YOU!!
HER DOOR IS CLOSED!

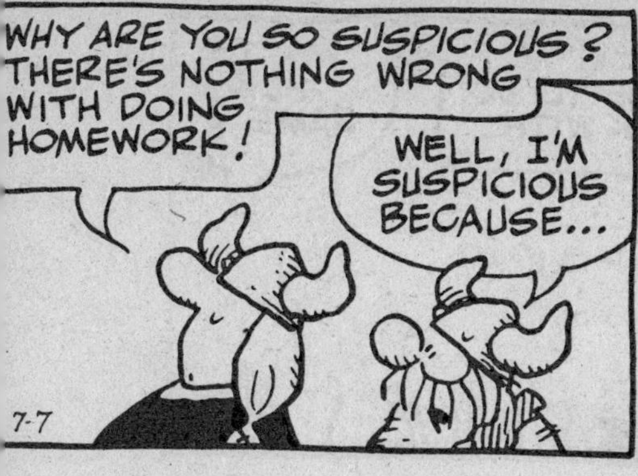
WHY ARE YOU SO SUSPICIOUS? THERE'S NOTHING WRONG WITH DOING HOMEWORK!
WELL, I'M SUSPICIOUS BECAUSE...
7-7

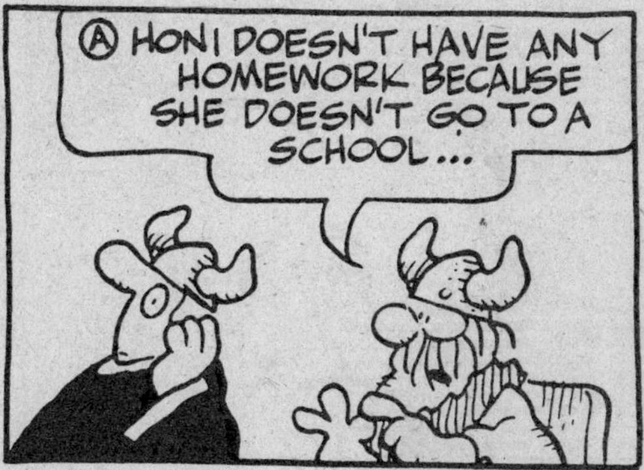
Ⓐ HONI DOESN'T HAVE ANY HOMEWORK BECAUSE SHE DOESN'T GO TO A SCHOOL...

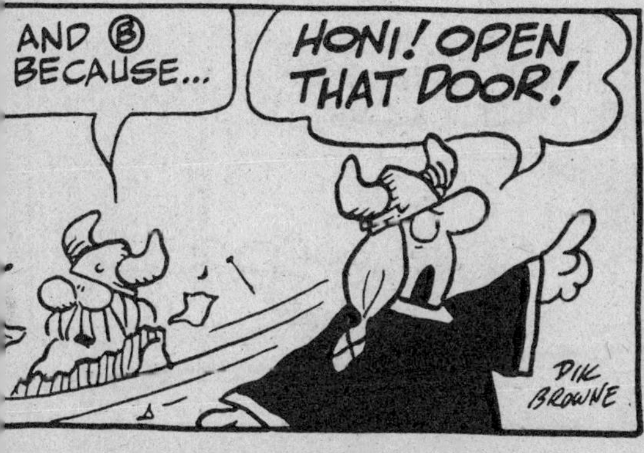
AND Ⓑ BECAUSE...
HONI! OPEN THAT DOOR!
DIK BROWNE

ALGAE

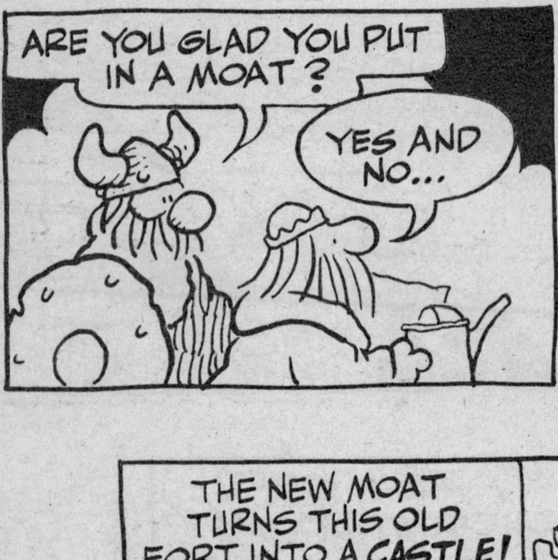
ARE YOU GLAD YOU PUT IN A MOAT?
YES AND NO...

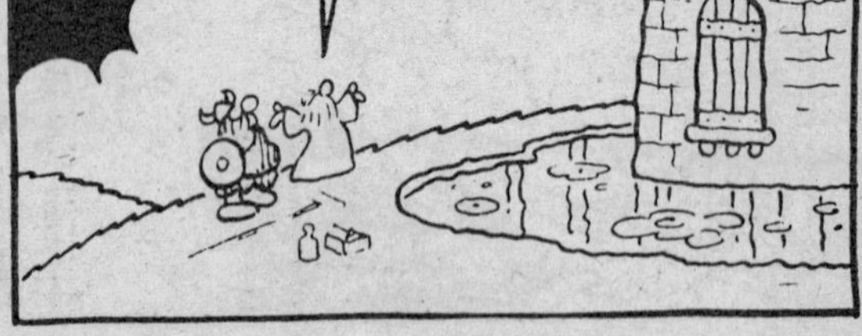
THE NEW MOAT TURNS THIS OLD FORT INTO A CASTLE!

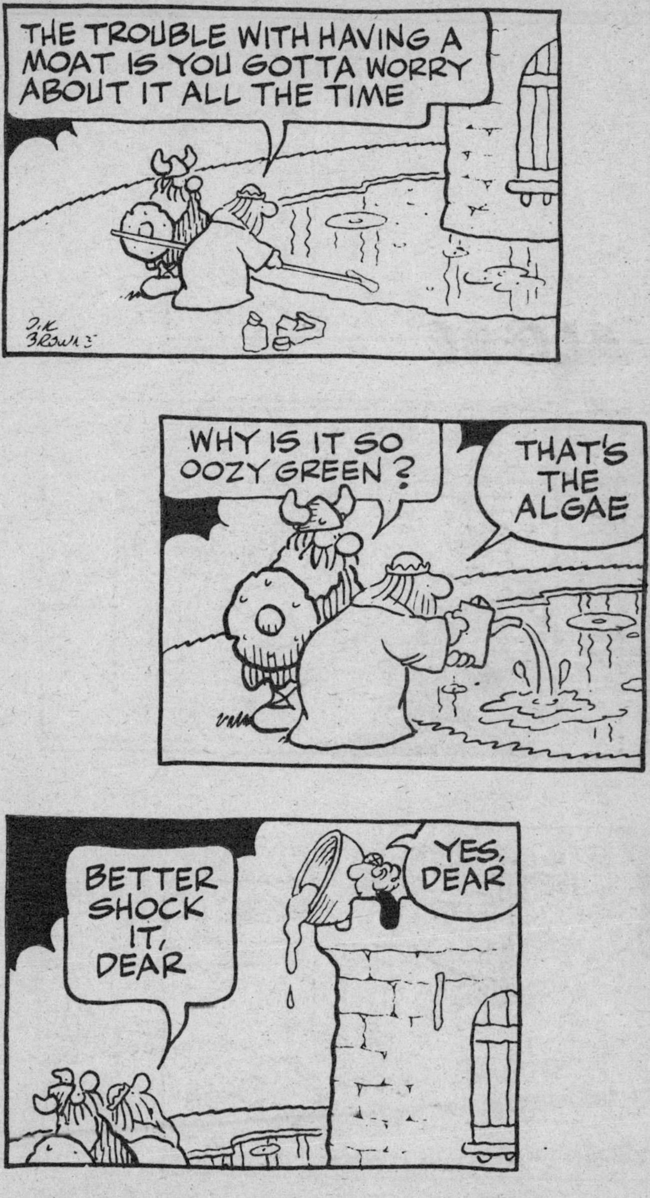
THE TROUBLE WITH HAVING A MOAT IS YOU GOTTA WORRY ABOUT IT ALL THE TIME
WHY IS IT SO OOZY GREEN?
THAT'S THE ALGAE
BETTER SHOCK IT, DEAR
YES, DEAR

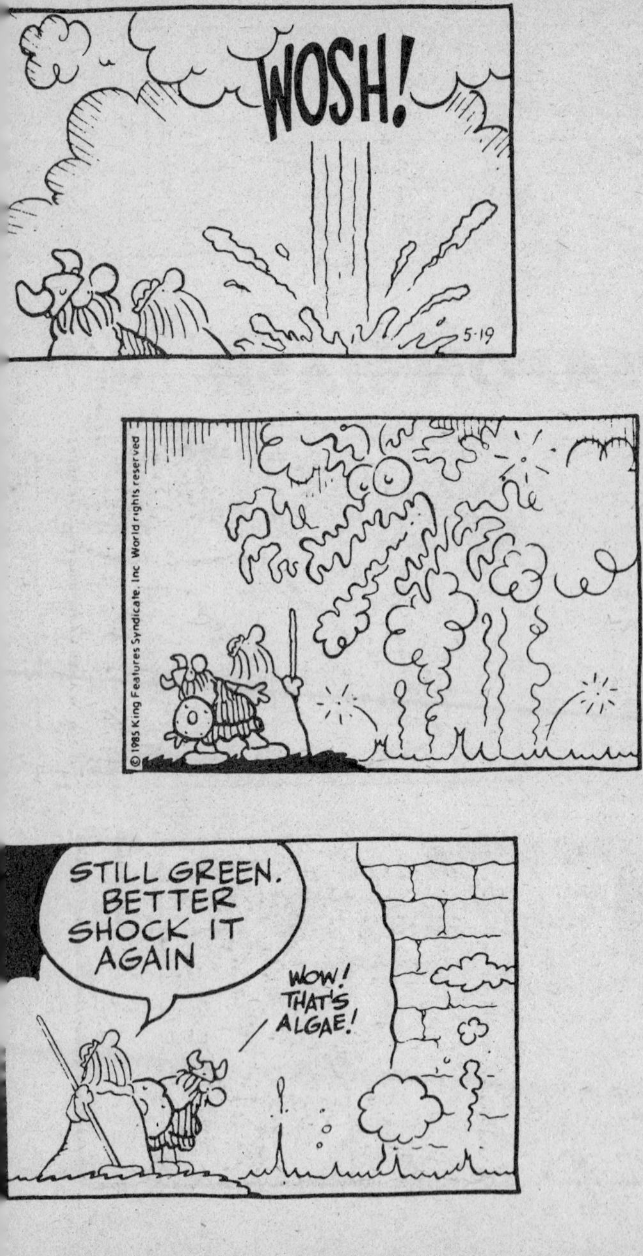
WOSH!
5-19
© 1985 King Features Syndicate, Inc. World rights reserved
STILL GREEN. BETTER SHOCK IT AGAIN
WOW! THAT'S ALGAE!

WEAPON WASH

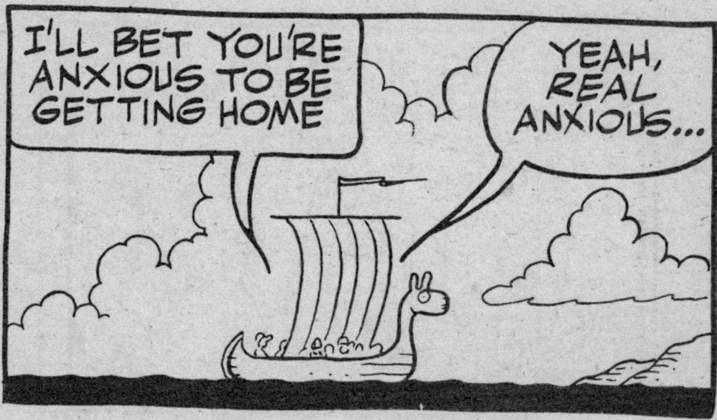
I'LL BET YOU'RE ANXIOUS TO BE GETTING HOME
YEAH, REAL ANXIOUS...

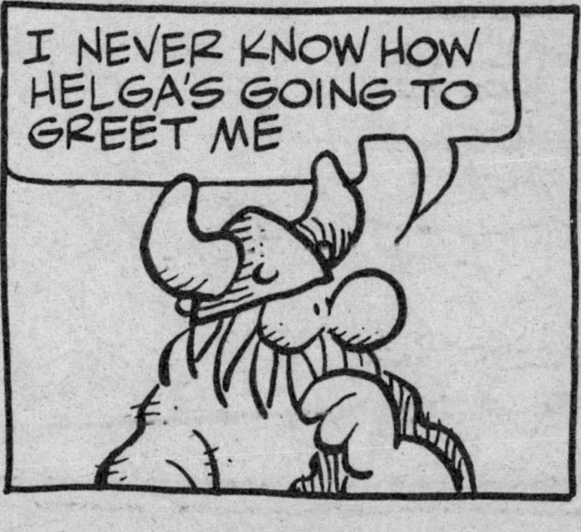
I NEVER KNOW HOW HELGA'S GOING TO GREET ME

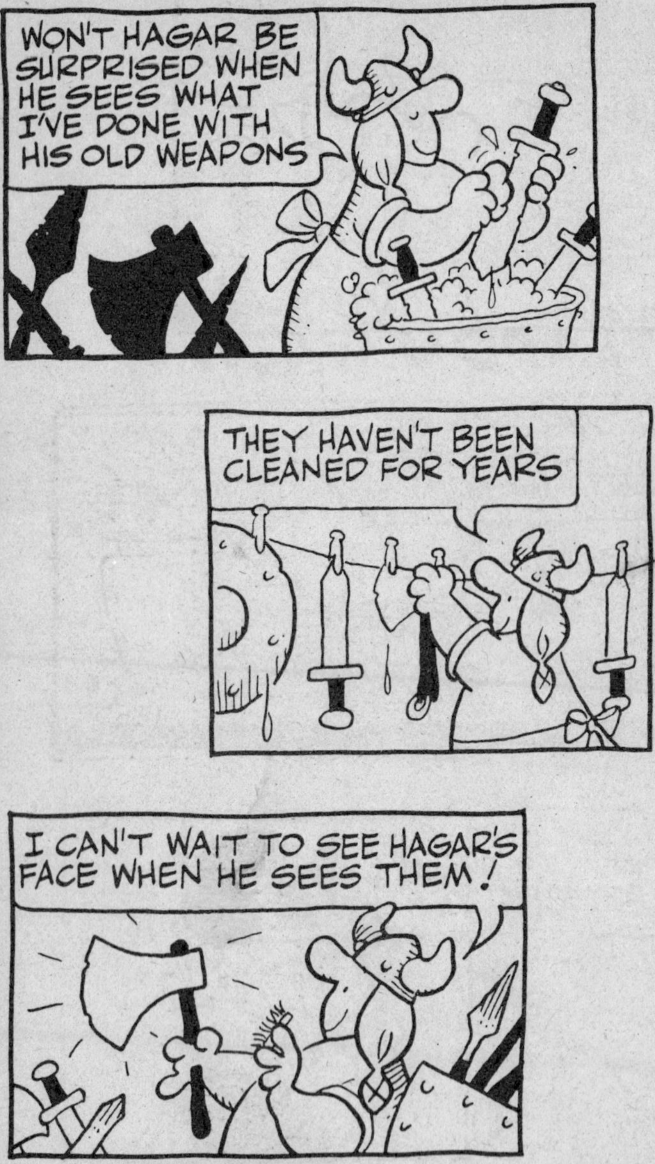
WON'T HAGAR BE SURPRISED WHEN HE SEES WHAT I'VE DONE WITH HIS OLD WEAPONS
THEY HAVEN'T BEEN CLEANED FOR YEARS
I CAN'T WAIT TO SEE HAGAR'S FACE WHEN HE SEES THEM!

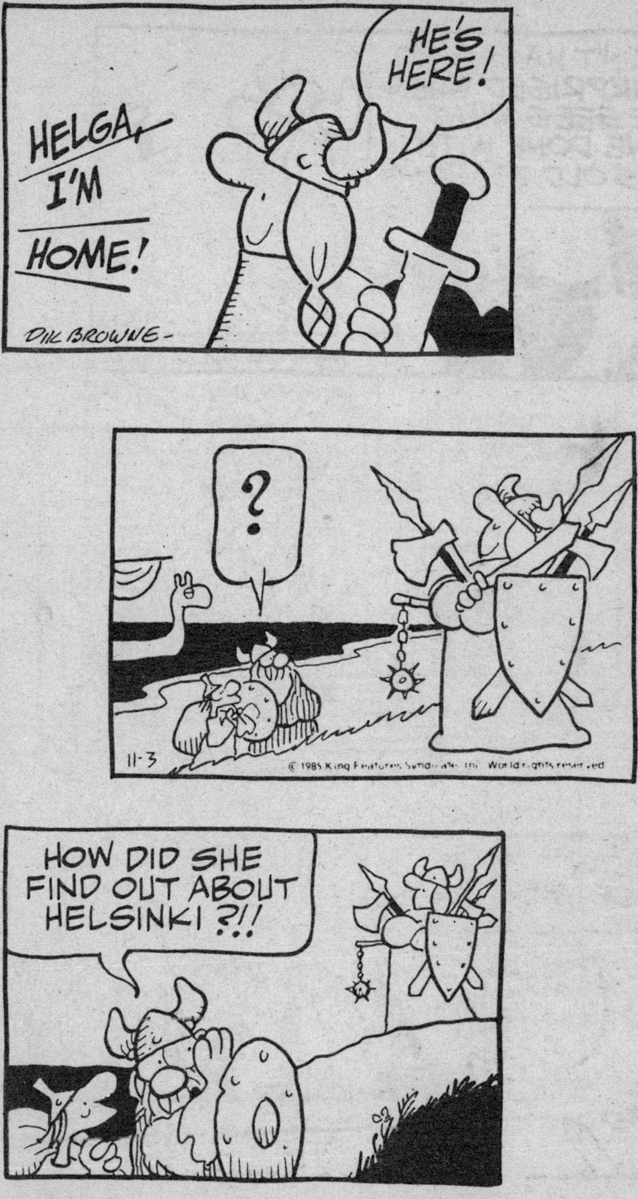
HELGA, I'M HOME!
HE'S HERE!
DIK BROWNE
?
11-3
© 1985 King Features Syndicate, Inc. World rights reserved
HOW DID SHE FIND OUT ABOUT HELSINKI ?!!

RARE HORNS

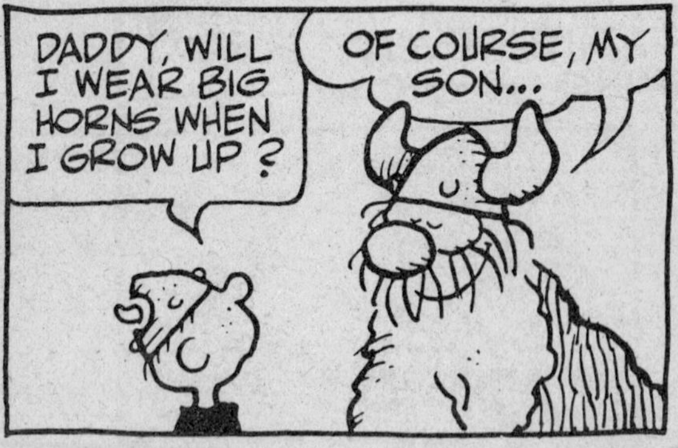
DADDY, WILL I WEAR BIG HORNS WHEN I GROW UP ?
OF COURSE, MY SON...

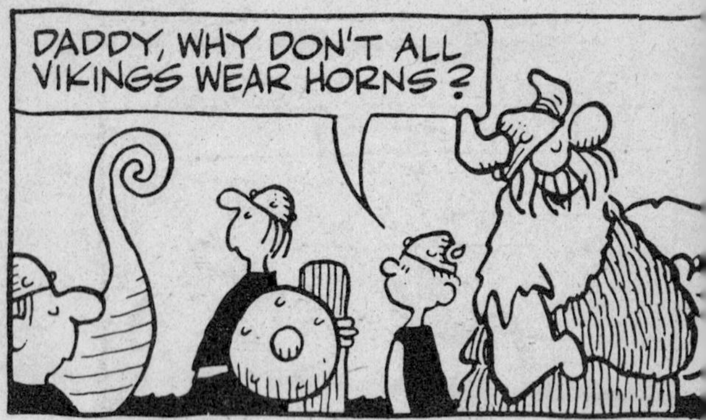
DADDY, WHY DON'T ALL VIKINGS WEAR HORNS ?

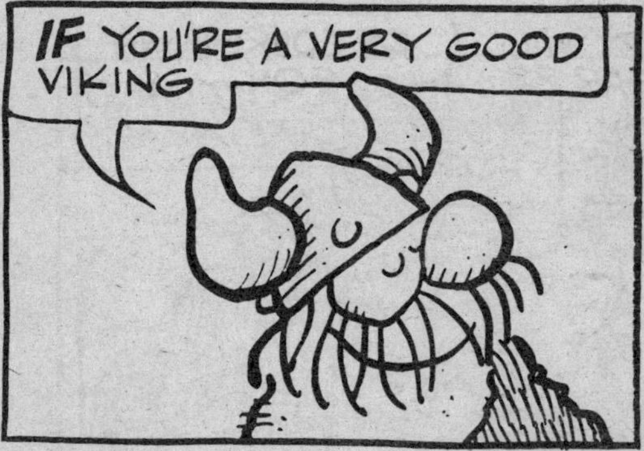
IF YOU'RE A VERY GOOD VIKING

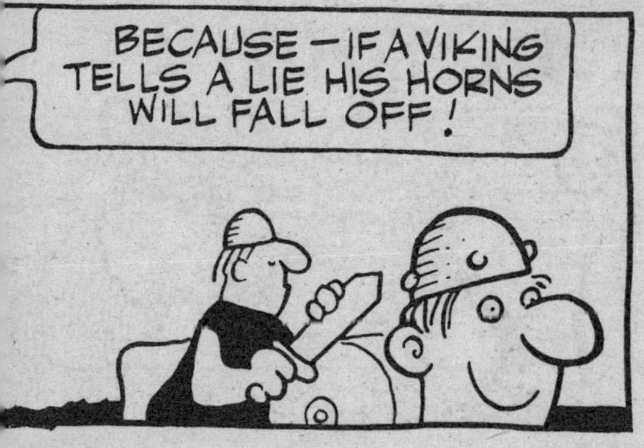
BECAUSE—IF A VIKING TELLS A LIE HIS HORNS WILL FALL OFF!

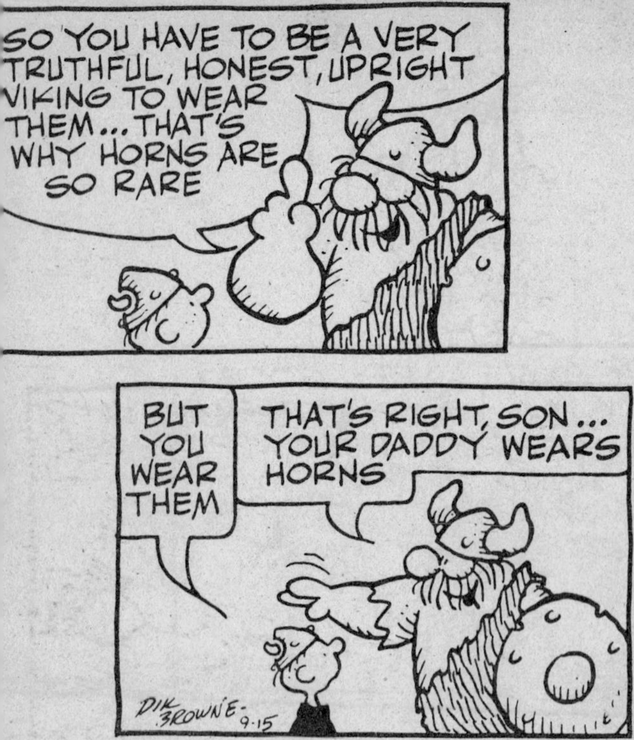
SO YOU HAVE TO BE A VERY TRUTHFUL, HONEST, UPRIGHT VIKING TO WEAR THEM... THAT'S WHY HORNS ARE SO RARE
BUT YOU WEAR THEM
THAT'S RIGHT, SON... YOUR DADDY WEARS HORNS
DIK BROWNE 9·15

AH, YOUTH!

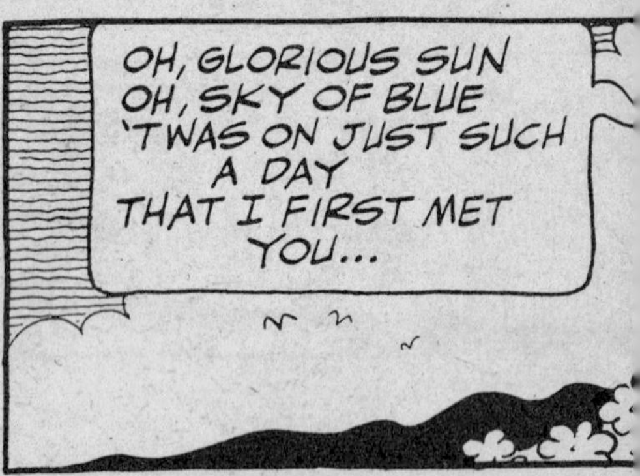
OH, GLORIOUS SUN OH, SKY OF BLUE 'TWAS ON JUST SUCH A DAY THAT I FIRST MET YOU...

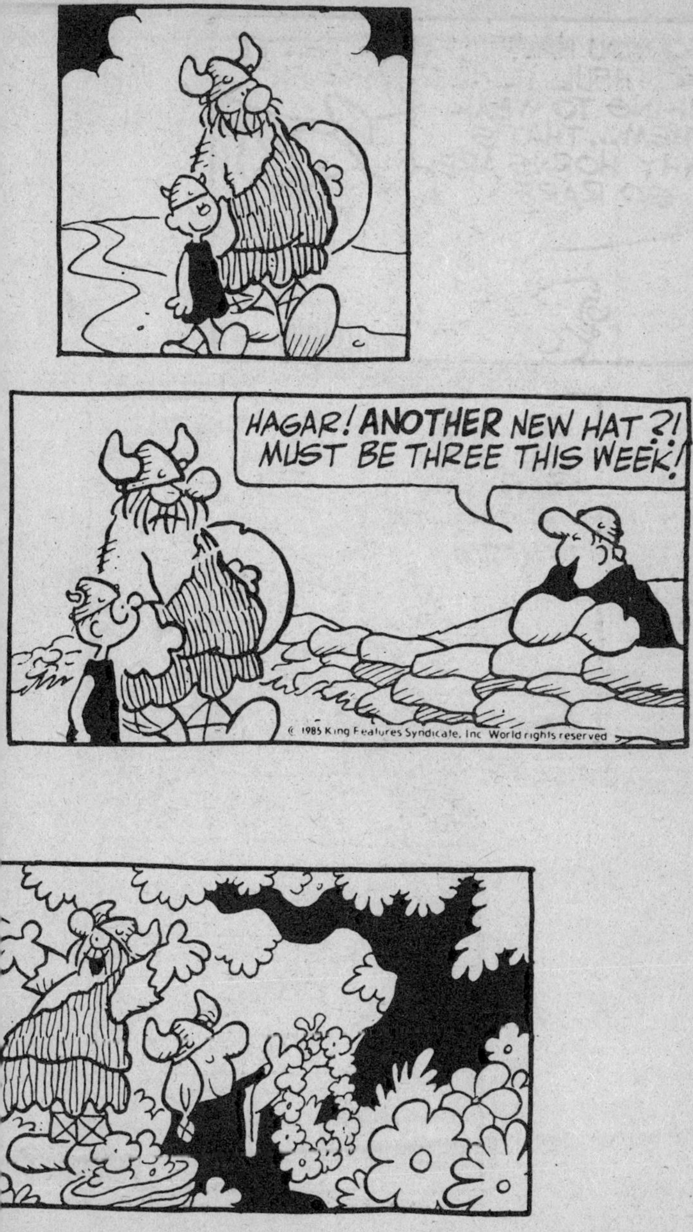
HAGAR! ANOTHER NEW HAT?! MUST BE THREE THIS WEEK!
© 1985 King Features Syndicate, Inc. World rights reserved

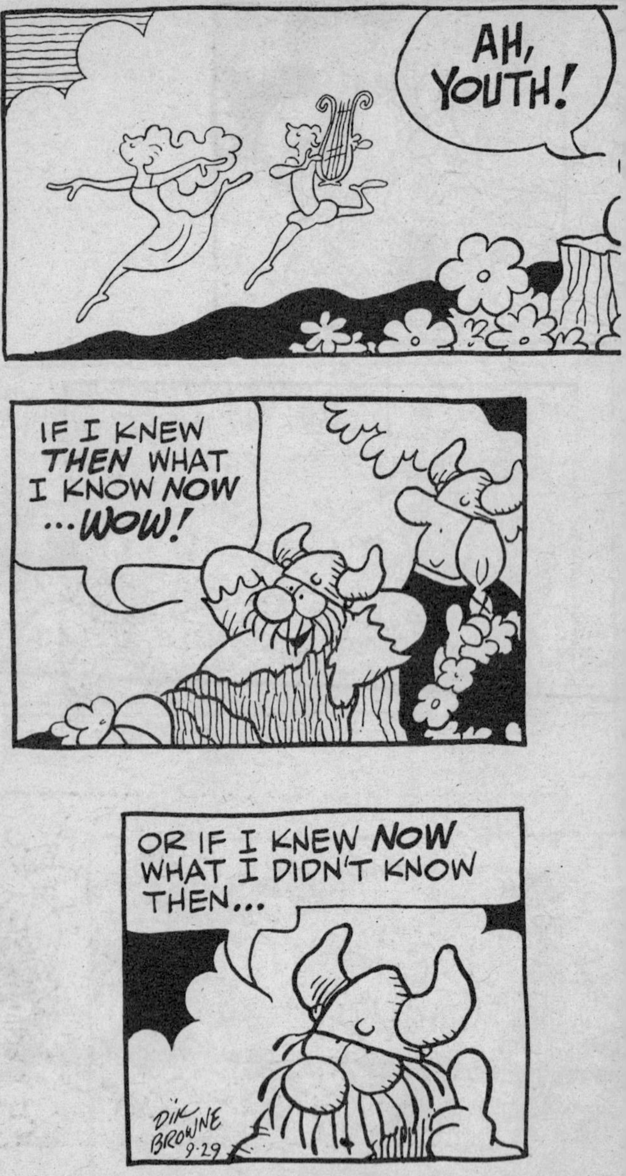
AH, YOUTH!
IF I KNEW THEN WHAT I KNOW NOW ...WOW!
OR IF I KNEW NOW WHAT I DIDN'T KNOW THEN...
DIK BROWNE 9·29

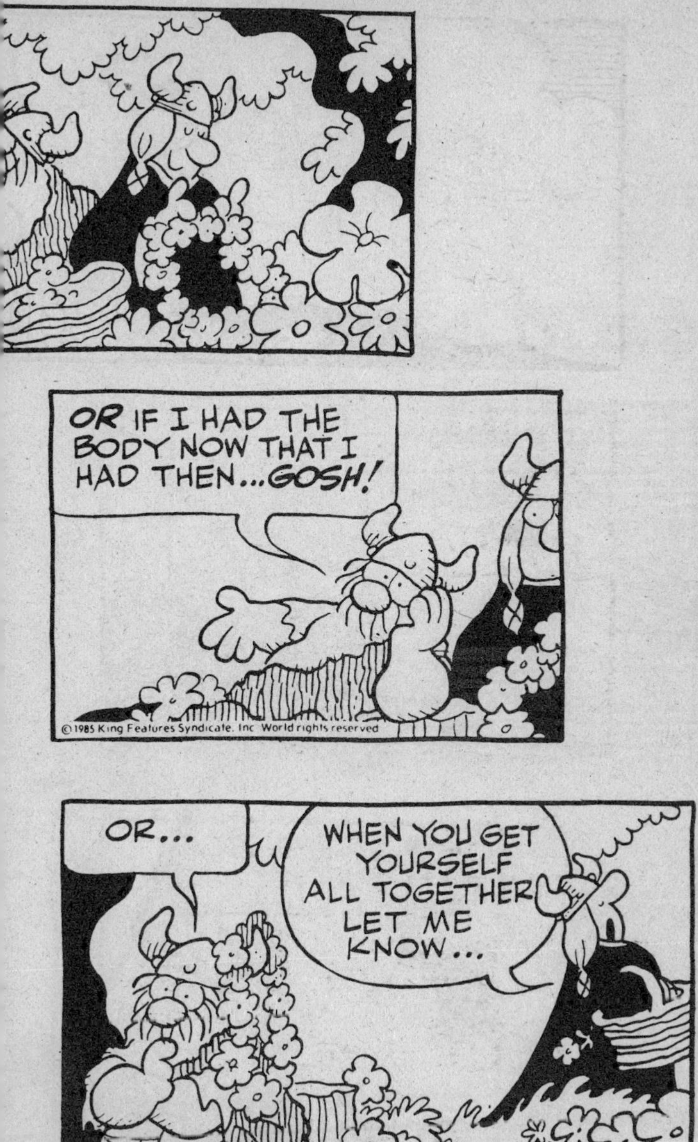
OR IF I HAD THE BODY NOW THAT I HAD THEN...GOSH!
© 1985 King Features Syndicate, Inc. World rights reserved
OR...
WHEN YOU GET YOURSELF ALL TOGETHER LET ME KNOW...

GREAT COOK

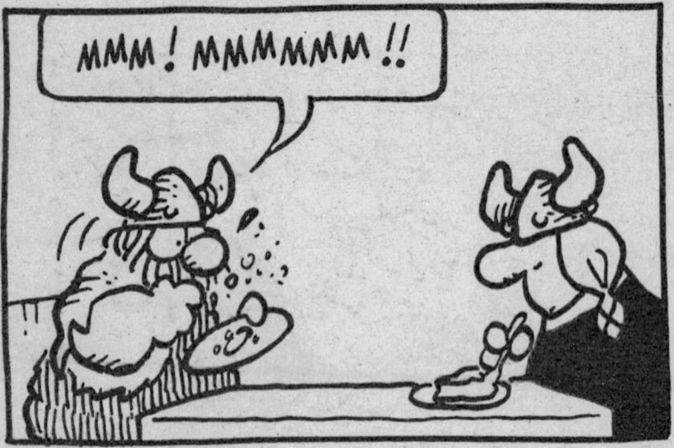
MMM! MMMMMM!!

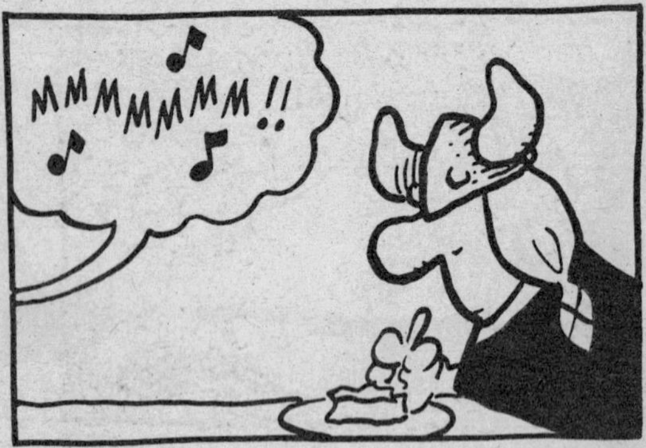
MMMMMMM!!

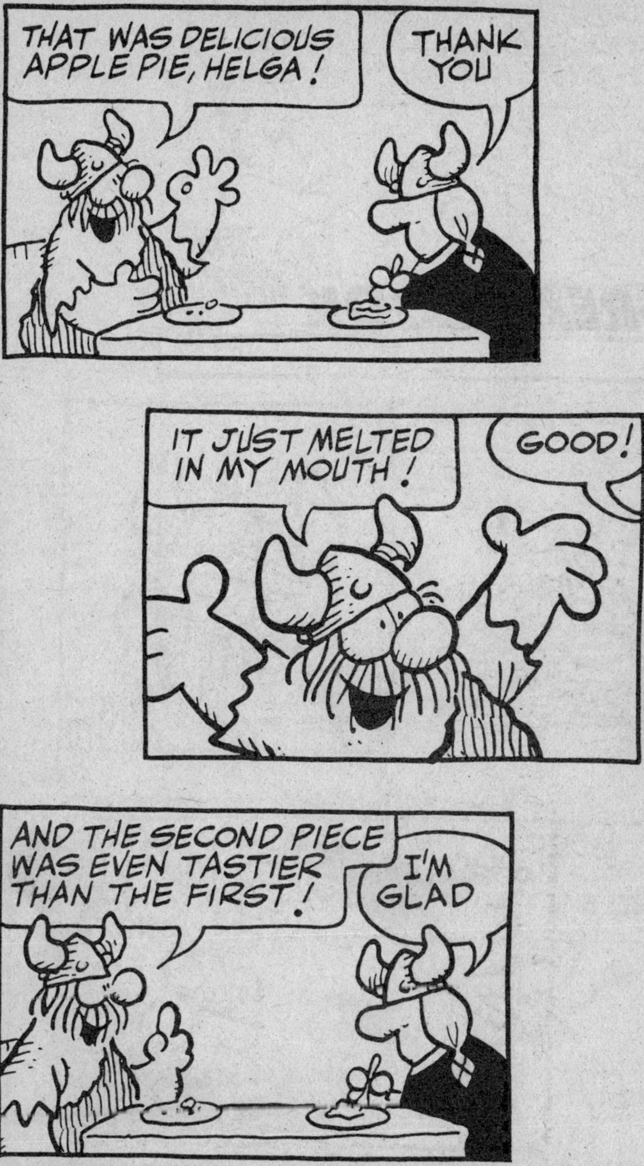
THAT WAS DELICIOUS APPLE PIE, HELGA!
THANK YOU
IT JUST MELTED IN MY MOUTH!
GOOD!
AND THE SECOND PIECE WAS EVEN TASTIER THAN THE FIRST!
I'M GLAD

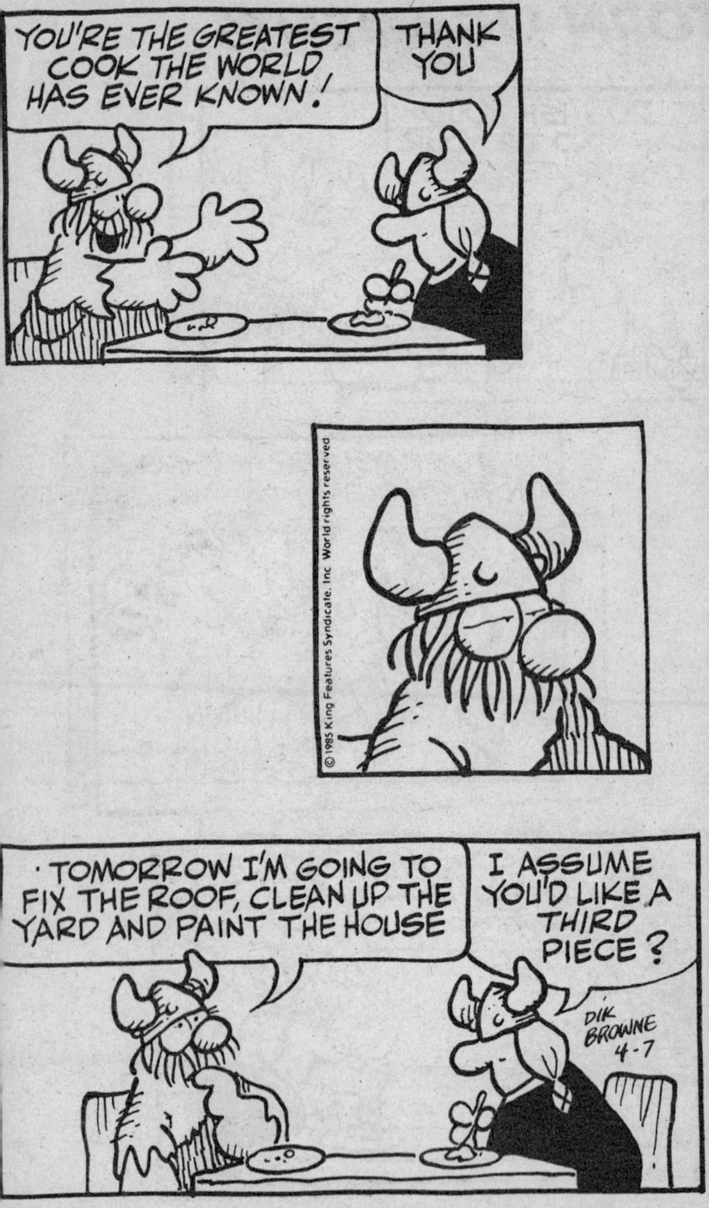
YOU'RE THE GREATEST COOK THE WORLD HAS EVER KNOWN!
THANK YOU
© 1985 King Features Syndicate, Inc World rights reserved
TOMORROW I'M GOING TO FIX THE ROOF, CLEAN UP THE YARD AND PAINT THE HOUSE
I ASSUME YOU'D LIKE A THIRD PIECE?
DIK BROWNE 4-7

TORN LIGAMENTS

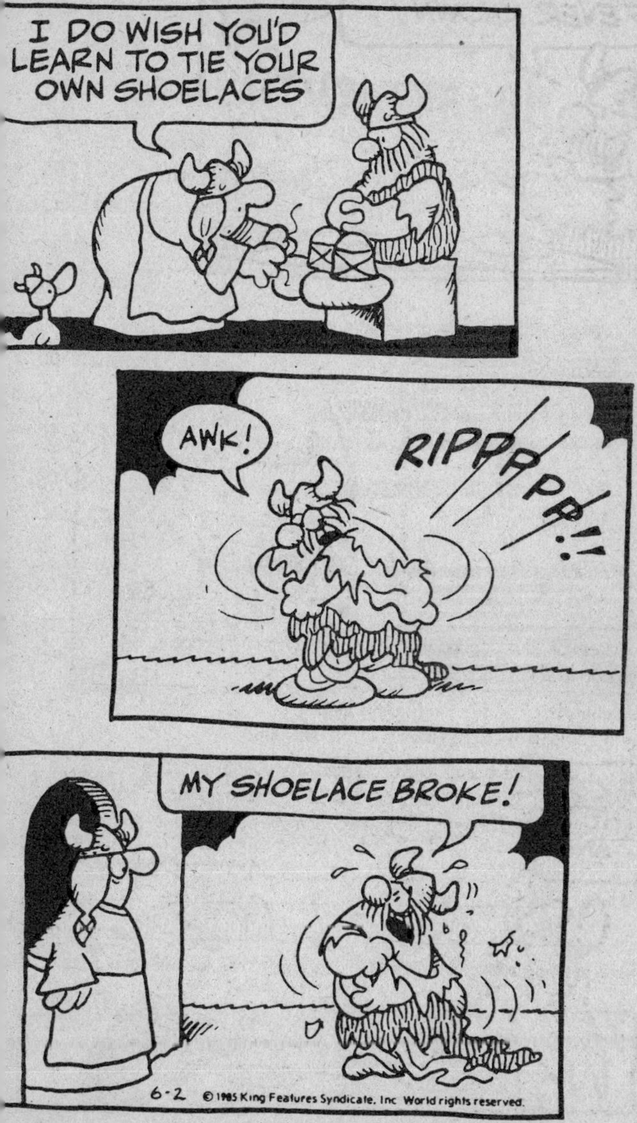
I DO WISH YOU'D LEARN TO TIE YOUR OWN SHOELACES
AWK!
RIPPPPPP!!!
MY SHOELACE BROKE!
6-2
© 1985 King Features Syndicate, Inc. World rights reserved.

HAGAR THE HORRIBLE

☐ 56762-5   HAGAR THE HORRIBLE: VIKINGS ARE FUN $2.95
☐ 56763-2   Canada $3.95

☐ 56790-0   HAGAR THE HORRIBLE: OUT ON A LIMB $1.95
☐ 56791-9   Canada $2.50

☐ 56788-9   HAGAR THE HORRIBLE: PILLAGE IDIOT $1.95
☐ 56789-7   Canada $2.50

☐ 56746-3   HAGAR THE HORRIBLE: $2.50
☐ 56747-1   ROOM FOR ONE MORE   Canada $3.50

☐ 50072-5   HAGAR: GANGWAY $2.95
☐ 50073-3   Canada $3.95

☐ 50560-3   HAGAR AND THE GOLDEN MAIDEN $2.95
☐ 50561-1   Canada $3.95

Buy them at your local bookstore or use this handy coupon:
Clip and mail this page with your order.

Publishers Book and Audio Mailing Service
P.O. Box 120159, Staten Island, NY 10312-0004

Please send me the book(s) I have checked above. I am enclosing $_____
(please add $1.25 for the first book, and $.25 for each additional book to
cover postage and handling. Send check or money order only—no CODs.)

Name _____

Address _____

City _____State/Zip _____

Please allow six weeks for delivery. Prices subject to change without notice.